"We're questing for Ms. Right, the ultimate partner," Chris said, getting caught up in her own fervor. "This isn't about booty. It's about true love."

"Is there such a thing?" B. said, getting teary.

"Yes," Chris said emphatically. She wasn't well qualified to speak on the subject but like any good evangelical speaker she could deliver the message and enthuse the follower. That, she knew was one of her strengths.

"You said we all have patterns. What do you think is my pattern?" Amadeus sipped her wine and sat down. She chose a barstool near the grill. She crossed her legs and looked mildly amused.

This was a loaded question. Chris smiled sweetly and replied, "We both have the same pattern. Two birds, one stone. Does 'flaky nymphomaniacs' ring any bells?"

Amadeus smiled. "I vote you president of the club."

Visit

Bella Books

at

BellaBooks.com

or call our toll-free number

1-800-729-4992

Date Night Club

Saxon Bennett

Bella
BOOKS

2007

Bella Books, Inc.
P.O. Box 10543
Tallahassee, FL 32302

Printed in the United States of America on acid-free paper
First Edition

Editor: Christi Cassidy
Cover designer: Stephanie Solomon-Lopez

ISBN-10: 1-59493-094-5
ISBN-13: 978-1-59493-094-2

*To my mom for inspiring me to write comedy
and embrace my inner quirk.*

Acknowledgment

To Ernie for all his funny stories without which life would seem bland.

About the Author

Saxon Bennett lives in the East Mountains with her beloved partner and her furry children, Sarah, Annie and Jane.

Chapter One

"Compatibility tests, my ass!" Chris McCoy said as she brought her black and chrome Harley Davidson to a screeching halt in front of the restaurant. The skid marks she left were impressive. She'd been stewing all afternoon. Ripping her backpack off, she pulled the offending magazine from inside. With some effort, she tore the magazine in half then quarters and finally into eighths. She let the pieces flutter in the breeze as they swirled and rolled their way down the street like errant children on their way to the park. Feeling much better, she walked to the entrance of her favorite restaurant, the Zoo. She planned to pick up dinner for herself and her friend Luce when a police car, lights flashing, pulled up.

A burly Hispanic police officer got out of the car. "Ma'am, what do you think you're doing?" He flipped open his slender black ticket book.

Chris ventured briefly into one of her favorite places—Smart Ass Land. *I'm going to get some dinner. Did you want me to buy you a doughnut? Or I'm going into a restaurant, you moron, what does it look like? Are you always this stupid or is today special?* Over the course of her thirty-five years on the planet, she'd learned that there are some people you just don't fuck with. Police officers fit snugly into this category.

Instead, she replied, "Excuse me, officer?"

"The magazine you ripped up," he replied.

Chris looked at his nametag, Officer Rivera. Between the car and the badge he appeared to be APD. She wasn't aware there were magazine police.

"Is there a law against the destruction of magazines?"

"No, but there is a law against littering."

"I wasn't littering. I was liberating myself from the bad vibes of my lover's compatibility test."

"No, you were littering. The mayor has come up with a stiff mandate on you people." He pulled his pen from his front pocket. "It's part of his campaign to clean up Albuquerque. You'll need to set a court date to explain your actions to the judge and receive your community service litter patrol time." He began writing the ticket. "Your name and address?"

"You can't be serious? I'll pick it up. It didn't even occur to me that I was littering. I'm just having a bad day."

"It's too late for that. Actions have consequences. Now, your personal information, please." He looked at her, his mouth curled downward under his thin mustache, his dark eyebrows knitted together so that his entire face was the epitome of disdain.

Chris relented. There was no worming and wiggling out of this one. She gave him her pertinent information, thinking the whole time that he reminded her of every authority figure she despised in her life, from the nuns at Catholic school to her hard-handed aunt who had raised her after her parents died in a freak accident. Her entire life was a serious of uncanny improbabilities laced in tragedy. This was par for the course.

"Now, Ms. McCoy, you have a nice evening," he said, before getting in the car and driving off to chastise other ne'er-do-wells.

Chris stomped into the restaurant and sat at the Martini Bar. The Zoo was famous for it's oversized seven-dollar martinis. She was contemplating having one while she waited for her takeout order when someone touched her thigh. She looked around and then down.

"I don't suppose you could give me a hand up," the midget asked.

"Of course." Chris got up and lifted the woman to the barstool. She wondered if the day could get any weirder, first a deceiving girlfriend, then a disdainful police officer and now a midget. She was beginning to feel like she was starring in a John Waters' film.

"Thank you. Did you sort out the thing with the police?" the woman asked.

"Yeah, I got a ticket for littering. I have to go to court and then pick up trash," Chris said. She studied the menu. She couldn't decide between the teriyaki chicken or the Bronco burger. The buns would get soggy by the time she got them to Luce's. The teriyaki chicken would travel better.

"Do you normally litter?"

Chris looked up from the menu. "No, I'm basically a tree-hugger type but my girlfriend—correction, ex-girlfriend—took this magazine quiz on compatibility and then started fucking her rock-climbing instructor. So I ripped up the magazine."

"I think you need my new invention."

"What's that? A mechanical heart that keeps love at bay?" Chris took a hard look at her. She was an attractive redhead, with short curly hair fashionably cut to just below her jaw. She had deep green eyes, a thin turned-up nose and lips that could model for Revlon. Aside from being three feet tall she looked like a quintessential Irish beauty.

"No, but that's not a bad idea. I was referring to a key-lime martini." Without waiting for Chris's response she waved down Rose, the bartender.

"Hey, Chris," Rose said, holding out her hand coiled in a fist so the two of them could bump knuckles. It was the hip version of hello, New Mexico style.

"Can you fix us up with two of my new martinis?" the woman asked.

"Sure. Those things are tasty. I had one myself last night. After work, of course," Rose said. Rose Ortega was a light-skinned Hispanic with black hair that hung to her shoulders. She had eyes like almonds and a very comely figure, large breasts and firm thighs. Chris liked to look at her.

"Oh, and Rose, can I put in a takeout order for the teriyaki chicken. I'm going to Luce's tonight and there's no food in Bumfuck."

"You're taking provisions. We have some really nice mince-meat tarts."

"Throw those in too. Thanks, Rose."

Rose winked at her. Both Chris and the midget watched her go.

"Oh, my," the woman said.

"Really?" Chris said incredulously.

"What? Midgets can't be lesbians?"

Chris laughed. "Oh, my God, I'm a size bigot. You'll have to forgive me."

"You're forgiven. It does take a bit getting used to."

Amadeus Holzkopf brought over the martinis. "Hello, Chris." They didn't bump knuckles. Amadeus was German and didn't like slang or strange hand signals. Her father, Dr. Holzkopf, had wanted a boy, but as fortune often does with a desire that runs too deep, his hopes were thwarted. He got a girl and gave her the boy's name he'd chosen. Amadeus grew up to be the son he always wanted. Chris thought it was like some creepy fairy tale. Amadeus owned the restaurant. The Zoo was all mahogany and high-class, a lot like its owner. "How are you?"

"I'm fine, thank you." Chris often felt like she was conversing with her sixth-grade English teacher, whom she had loathed. Mrs. Adel ate white powdered doughnuts, which stuck to her red lipstick, and found great amusement in terrifying her students into grammatical precision.

"I see you've met Midge."

Chris had just taken a sip of her drink, which she spewed over the mahogany bar. "Sorry. It was kind of a shock."

Amadeus grabbed a bar towel and wiped up the bar, giving Chris a reprimanding look.

Midge said, "No problem. I just figured that since it was a nickname people gave me I would claim it as my own."

"Taking your identity into your own hands," Chris said. "It's fitting. Look at Amadeus. She fits her name."

"Meaning?" Amadeus inquired as she straightened out her black brocade vest.

"Well, you're a lovely, blue-eyed, red-haired German amazon."

This time Midge laughed.

"And your name, what does it tell us?" Amadeus asked.

"That I am one of a hundred thousand million Chrises in the world and I hold no distinction."

"When I think of the name Chris, I think of that sitcom. We used to watch it in Germany. It was called *Three's Company*. That blond woman that played Chrissy. Women named Chris seem to be attractive blue-eyed blondes with nice figures."

"And no brains," Chris added.

Amadeus smirked. "I didn't say that."

"But she's right. You are hot," Midge said.

Chris blushed. "Thanks, Midge. You're doing wonders for my fragile self-image."

"Any time. How's your drink?"

"It's fabulous," Chris said, taking another sip.

There was shrieking from the kitchen. Amadeus rolled her eyes. "My pastry chef will be the death of me."

"You shouldn't have banged her," Chris said.

"That's ugly American slang. Besides, you are the queen of poor choices and have absolutely no room to talk." Amadeus stomped off in the direction of the kitchen.

"I don't think she's happy with you," Midge said.

Chris let out a heavy sigh. "I'm having a really fucked-up day. I should keep my mouth shut."

The restaurant was filling up for the happy hour. Rose brought Chris her order. "I threw in a few extras. Tell Luce hi for me."

"Thanks, Rose." Chris finished her martini.

"It was nice to meet you, Chris," Midge said, holding out her knuckles. "And I hope to see you again."

"I hang here all the time," Chris said, her knuckles touching Midge's.

"Then so shall I."

Once outside, Chris pushed the starter and her bike rumbled to life. She gave the throttle a few quick turns and then took off. It was the first of May and already summer was in full swing. The days were warmer and longer. Chris liked that. It meant wearing less clothing and riding in the light. The Sandia Mountains were bathed in the watermelon glow they had been named for. The city was nestled at the foot of the mountains. Chris headed up Central toward Tramway Boulevard. She took the back way to Luce's house in Placitas. The interstate always got jammed up in rush hour traffic, so Chris had become adept at finding alternate routes.

The shops of the Nob Hill area were closing and the bars

were opening up. Nob Hill and the University District were full of hip shops, bars and restaurants that catered to the eclectic and wealthy in Albuquerque's Northeast Heights. They also catered to the impoverished university student with a few bucks left over. It was an odd mix of rich and intelligently poor. Chris window-shopped as she waited for the string of lights that controlled traffic. Each block had one and they were not sequenced. Everyone coming this way window-shopped while they waited. She'd never stopped in any of the stores. She'd only looked in and wondered at the contents. Maybe one day she'd talk Luce into going shopping with her, now that she had rid herself of yet another nut-ball girlfriend. They could wander aimlessly through Nob Hill and then have lunch somewhere.

She finally hit Tramway and let the bike run. She made it from Central to the dirt road that led up to Luce's house in twenty-five minutes. She was a fast rider and had great anticipatory skills. She was good at deducing which asshole was going to cut her off. This was a life-saving measure in the world of motorcycle riders.

Luce met her out in the driveway. She'd been crossing from the studio to the house when Chris arrived. Luce's art studio was a fascinating place, full of tools, wood saws for making frames, and pieces of colored glass, all housed in a large A-frame building. She had picked some early blooming purple bearded iris and they lay across her arms. She was wearing a long green skirt with a white blouse tied up around her waist. It was no wonder her ex-lover Claire had fallen in love with Luce, Chris mused as she pulled off her helmet.

Luce had brown hair effortlessly sun-streaked that fell down to the middle of her back and that she wore in an array of complex styles—French-braided, up in bun, twirled together and tied in some amazing knot or pulled back with a strand or two hanging about her face. It amazed Chris, who got her short hair cut every six weeks in one of seven known lesbian hairstyles.

Luce had large dark eyes with long eyelashes, a thin aristocratic nose and high cheekbones. Her lips were full and well curved. As with her hair, she played with a wide assortment of looks—skirts, blazers, jeans, boots, sandals or runners—and looked great in everything.

"I should have brought flowers for the hostess," Chris said, nodding at the irises.

"You brought the food and you think flowers are overrated," Luce replied.

"Are you implying I'm not romantic?"

"Yes."

"Well, you'd be right, but I like what you do with the flowers." She was referring to Luce's creative abilities. Luce worked in stained glass. She made huge pieces that hung in corporate offices and in the homes of CEOs. Her work was abstract, so what started as flowers when filtered through Luce's mind became something more. Chris thought of it as art on LSD.

Luce gave Chris a hug, wrapping her arms and the flowers around her so that she felt engulfed in scents, Luce's and the irises. She'd always had an affinity for Luce. When Claire dumped her for Luce, she'd been certain Luce would immediately hop in bed with her. After all, Claire was now a successful writer. But before Luce would have anything to do with her sexually she had to make restitution with Chris. Claire was to purchase Chris a house in repayment for the seven years of support she'd given Claire while she worked on her novel. Chris always referred to it as the "blood-money house." For as angry as she was with Claire, she ended up liking Luce. Claire had been careful to keep them separated but after she died Chris and Luce had become best friends.

"Sophie called."

"She did?" Chris feigned ignorance.

"She was crying. She said you threw her out of the house."

Chris backed away and busied herself pulling dinner out of

the fanny pack on her bike. She didn't want to talk about it. She peeked inside the bag. The Styrofoam containers appeared intact. There were two extra. Chris smiled, remembering that Rose had put some surprises in.

"Chris?" Luce prompted.

"It had to be done."

"Any particular reason?" Luce asked as they walked toward the old adobe house.

"She was banging her rock-climbing instructor at my house during lunch. She told Helga that I was her roommate."

"How original," Luce said, opening the French doors that led in from the veranda to the kitchen.

"We had a little chat. Sophie had gone back to work and I found Helga getting out of the shower. I asked her how many times she got Sophie to come."

"Chris!"

"She said three. Not bad for a nooner."

"So you threw Sophie out." Luce pulled the food from the bag and dished it onto plates. It was teriyaki chicken, jasmine rice, cream-cheese-filled croissants, a mixed green salad with Caesar dressing and the mincemeat tarts.

"Yep, I packed her shit in a cardboard box and set it on the porch, then I changed the locks."

"Busy lunch hour."

"I had to take an hour of annual to cover it. My supervisor, Sid, was very understanding. He found out his wife is doing the cable guy, and meanwhile he hasn't had ESPN for months."

Luce set the oven on low and put the plates inside. She thought microwaves were evil and did bad things to your brain. She didn't have one. Instead she purchased dishware that was oven-safe and used the oven for everything. Chris felt like she should turn her own microwave into a terrarium so Luce would believe her commitment to a cleaner, safer planet.

"Let's sit out back and have a glass of wine while the food

warms up. I got a great bottle of Pinot Noir at Trader Joe's the other day," Luce said, taking two glasses from the rack on the wall.

"Sure. Let me open it. I need to practice."

"All right, but if you run into trouble you have to stop. I'm not going to spend the rest of the evening picking pieces of cork out of my wineglass."

"I've been watching the Food Network. I think I've got it down," Chris said, taking the corkscrew Luce gave her. She lined it up perfectly in the center and gave it a jab, tested it to make sure it stuck and gave the corkscrew two quick turns, then she yanked. The cork came out perfectly.

Luce clapped. "You did it."

"I may not be the sharpest tool in the shed but I am trainable."

"That you are." Luce poured the wine and they went out back.

The veranda of Luce's house was enclosed with a slatted roof covered with purple wisteria that had grown up the support posts. Its leaves and purple cone-like flowers hung in bunches between the slats. Chris always felt like she was sitting in a secret arbor hidden from the world, sipping wine with her best friend in the chic Scandinavian chairs Luce bought at IKEA. The patio was paved in a faded orange flagstone. Giant pots of flowers and herbs, along with pieces of stone sculpture, were placed throughout. It looked like one of those garden oasis photos Chris saw on the cover of the spring issue of *Sunset* magazine.

They had a perfect view of the Sandia Mountains and the dotted landscape full of juniper trees and scrub that lay before it. The watermelon glow had melted away and the twinkling lights of the foothill houses were flickering as twilight approached. Soon the sky would be pierced with stars. It was nice to get out of the city, Chris thought as she sat back in her chair and sipped her wine. She forgot about her lousy day. That is, until Luce brought it up.

"Chris, why do you hang out with women like that?"

"Because she was a nymphomaniac and after that debacle with Monique, who only puts out to hook up and then locks the box, I wanted something different. If I was going to go through the pain of having a girlfriend I'd like one that gives it up. You could look at Sophie just right and she'd hop on you."

"And the rock-climbing instructor must have looked at her just right."

"You can say that again."

"When are you going to hook up with someone meaningful?"

"Never. They all cheat. It's not like I'm a total loser. It really pisses me off. I'm not that bad."

Luce smile and took her hand. "No, you're not."

"How about you? I think the appropriate grieving time has passed."

Luce stared out at the darkening horizon. She lit a candle the size of a dessert plate sitting on the table next to her. The candle smelled of citronella. Chris wondered what she was thinking. Was it a good memory of Claire, one where she was smiling and content in the moment? Or after making love when her eyes seemed restful as Luce held her in her arms? Or was it the flaming car after it went around Dead Man's Curve on Old Route 66 and smashed into the bank? There wasn't enough left of her to put in an urn, as if she couldn't give either one of them anything to remember her by. What a selfish bitch, Chris thought.

Luce broke Chris's mental tirade—thinking ill of the dead. She'd probably go to some special place in hell for that. "I just wondered if she would have been better off with you."

Chris balked. "Not on your life. I was never good enough for her. You know Claire was happiest with you. I'm not creative. I'm not tormented with an ideal that is unachievable. I'm just here. I like to ride my motorcycle. I like good food. I like my friends. I like a stiff drink and a slow easy fuck at the end of the day. How's that for simple?"

Luce laughed.

"What are you thinking?"

"That I wish I could get her out of my head. This solitary life is not all it's cracked up to be."

"You have me to break the tedium," Chris offered.

"Maybe now that you're unattached we could play more."

"I'd like that. I want to go shopping in Nob Hill in all those stores I look at but never go in."

"It's a date then. Let's go eat. It should be warm by now."

"Luce," Chris said, catching her arm. "If you ever need anything, you'd tell me, right?"

"I'm not as dramatic or as drastic as Claire. I'd go to Nepal and make prayer flags if I got desperate."

"Some of those nuns are hot."

"Chris!"

She laughed and they went inside. "There's one on my route. Kelsang Prahad . . . or something like that, and she's cute."

"Tell me some your stories. They always make me laugh," Luce said. She set the table and lit the candelabra in the center.

"There's this one guy . . ." Chris began, knowing she'd spend the rest of the evening making Luce laugh.

Chapter Two

"I love this place," Midge said. "The dark mahogany tables, the white canvas chairs, the Ernest Hemingway feel—hunting white elephants, big-gun safari thing. I mean, she's even got Queen Palms growing in the atrium."

"Wow, that was a mouthful," Chris said as she slurped the end of her martini. "I like the eye candy. The tropical safari thing is fine, odd for a German to choose, but then, naming the place the Zoo is just as fucking weird."

"Eye candy?" Midge inquired. She waved at Rose for two more key-lime martinis.

"Attractive women."

"Oh, yes, there is that."

They both turned to look at a well-dressed, handsome woman who cruised by. She was a leggy brunette in an Ann Taylor business suit, her white blouse cut sufficiently low.

"Speaking of which, how is your newly single life going?"

"I've been hanging out with Luce. Cinco de Mayo was kind of slow. You know, usually it's chilis rellenos, margaritas and a lot of salsa in the sack. We did go shopping in Nob Hill. I bought a couple of beanbag chairs. I love those things. I threw them in the den."

"So Luce used to date Claire who used to date you."

"Yeah, something like that."

Chris ordered two more drinks. Rose swung them by quickly, given that happy hour was hopping, and winked at her.

"Claire was the writer that died in the car crash."

"Yeah." Chris pretended to be engrossed in her new drink.

"But you don't like to talk about it."

"Midge, where's this going? It's over with. So what's the point of rehashing it?"

"Because sometimes when you talk about things instead of burying them you can move on. You could find someone decent instead of the bimbos you've been hanging out with."

"Have you been talking to Amadeus?" Chris sipped her drink and eyed Midge suspiciously.

"She may have mentioned a few things."

"Like she has any room to talk."

"Point well taken."

"So what's your story?"

"I'm just hanging out waiting for the perfect midget to come along and sweep me off my feet."

Chris laughed so hard she nearly fell off her barstool.

"I know, silly me." Midge smiled at her coyly.

Chris wiped her eyes with a cocktail napkin. "I'm sorry. Do you have an aversion to people of height?"

"Sometimes. I like you, though."

"Thanks, Midge."

"I left Dallas to get away from this woman. She was really

jealous and I didn't like being treated like someone's teddy bear. I want a sane relationship."

"I get it."

They sipped their martinis in companionable silence until suddenly the screaming and wailing started. It was coming from the kitchen.

"Three guesses," Chris said.

"The pastry chef and Amadeus," Midge replied.

"Bingo."

The lanky brunette pastry chef, Shirley, came flying out the stainless steel kitchen doors wielding a rolling pin and screaming, "I quit."

"You can't quit. You're fired," Amadeus screamed back.

Shirley marched past them.

Amadeus stood in the middle of the bar with her hands on her hips and shaking her head. "Good riddance."

There was a loud crash outside the restaurant, and then another and another. Amadeus looked over at Chris and Midge. They all made for the front door. Shirley was smashing the back window of Amadeus's black 325i BMW. There was glass everywhere. She hit the hood and front panels next. Amadeus stood stunned. There was going to be nothing left of the car. Midge snapped open her cell phone and dialed 911.

"At least my bimbo girlfriends aren't vindictive," Chris said. She was still miffed that Amadeus had been talking behind her back to Midge.

"I loved that car," Amadeus said.

Two squad cars pulled up. One of the officers grabbed the rolling pin just before he got clocked with it. An attractive female office got out and helped her partner restrain and hand-cuff the assailant.

"What's going on here?" the female officer asked.

"She won't live with me. She won't let me live with her. I

thought we loved each other," Shirley blubbered. "All she loves is that fucking car."

"Whose car is this?" the male officer asked.

"It was mine," Amadeus said, starting to tear up, her eyes reddening.

Chris searched her pockets for a tissue. All she came up with was a crumpled ATM receipt. She wondered if she had entered it in her check register. Midge produced a neatly folded linen hanky. Amadeus nodded her thanks.

"See? Look at her. She cries for the car but not for me," Shirley shrieked. She lunged for Amadeus. The cops grabbed her and shoved her unceremoniously into the squad car.

The female office, Elaine Rodriguez, as her nametag indicated, came over to talk to Amadeus. "So I take it you two had a falling-out."

Amadeus nodded and continued to stare at her car with its gaping holes for windows, smashed headlights and dented hood.

"She does this all the time. She thinks of these relationships as brief encounters but lesbians don't think like that. At minimum, a one-night stand equals love at first sight and a one-year commitment," Chris jabbered. She felt someone tug at her pant leg. She looked down. It was Midge.

"Could I talk to you for a minute over there?" Midge said, pointing into thin air ten paces away.

"Sure."

When they were alone, Chris squatted down so she could be eye level with Midge.

"You don't have to do that."

"I know but I prefer it. If I was crotch level all the time I'd be horribly distracted."

Midge laughed. "Yes, I'm afraid you would be. I don't think you're helping Amadeus's case by making her out to be a femme fatale. That is a very expensive sports car that a scorned woman with a rolling pin destroyed."

Chris furrowed her brow and thought about it for a moment. She did have a point. Her chagrin faded. It hadn't been right of Amadeus to make value judgments about her relationship with Claire or other women, but retribution was a fine leveler. She could muster some empathy. "I'll keep my trap shut."

"Thank you."

When they returned Amadeus had finished giving her statement and Shirley had been hauled off. Amadeus called her insurance agent. It wasn't going well. "Just come and look at the fucking auto. Then you'll understand." She clicked off. The business transactions done, it appeared she was cascading through the various stages of grief—sadness turned to anger.

Chris and Midge watched.

"Not only is my car ruined but I'm out a pastry chef." She sighed heavily.

"I could probably help," Midge offered.

"What, you just happen to be a pastry chef?" Chris said.

"As a matter of fact, I am. Sarah K. Roswell at your service," Midge said, curtsying.

Amadeus put on her thinking face, which meant she drew her eyes down and pursed her lips. It was a very unappealing pose, Chris thought.

"As in Roswellian Puff Pastry, now sold in better grocery stores everywhere," Amadeus said.

"You're a rich midget," Chris said.

Midge shrugged. "I have a good business manager. Besides, I'm technically retired. Although I am on the board."

"What the hell is Roswellian Puff Pastry?" Chris asked.

"Oh, my goodness, it's to die for," Amadeus said.

"You'll have to try one," Midge said, her modest demeanor completely unchanged.

"You would do that for me?" Amadeus said.

"Of course. I'm going to need an assistant this evening." Midge looked over at Chris.

"I've been a busboy, the dishwasher, the cashier and once I was a waiter."

"But she was rude and I had to remove her from the floor," Amadeus added.

"That woman had no right to be so condescending," Chris said.

Amadeus waved her hand and rolled her eyes. "She lacks the proper hypocrisy for public service."

"I'm in public service. What the hell do you think the mailman is?"

"People expect rudeness from the government," Amadeus replied.

"Well, anyway, I'd love to be your assistant. I work for food," Chris said, looking pointedly at Amadeus.

"You do come in handy in a crisis," Amadeus conceded. She held out her fist in apology. Chris bumped knuckles with her and thought perhaps the car-beating episode might be good for Amadeus.

"Let me go get my stuff from the van," Midge said.

"Can I help?" Chris offered.

"Sure."

Chris touched Amadeus's shoulder. "I'm sorry about your car."

"I'm sorry I spoke ill of your girlfriends."

Chris went with Midge to her van where Midge handed her a black leather bag and a set of metal stilts that construction workers used to install drywall. "What the hell do you need these for?"

"Restaurant kitchens are not adapted for small people. These put me at just the right level."

"Wow, that's a great idea."

Chris was inducted into the kitchen, given an apron and put to work. The pastry kitchen had its own alcove set off from the rest of the busy kitchen. In the center of the alcove was a large granite-covered table where the dough was laid out. Off to one side was a set of sinks, racks of trays and bowls and on the other side a set of ovens and a large range. Midge set out the bowls and pans she would need and set forth gathering ingredients from the pantry. She mixed while Chris handed her the dry goods. When she was done they would start making the pastry. Once they got the pastry in the oven they went out to the bar to get a glass of ice water.

"I forgot how hot it gets working in the kitchen," Chris said, as she poured them both a large glass from the pitcher Amadeus kept behind the bar.

"It brings back pleasant memories from my youth," Midge said.

"Right," Chris replied.

They were both chugging down a second glass when Luce showed up.

"What on earth happened to Amadeus's Beemer?" Luce asked.

Chris smiled and said, "The pastry chef." She came around the bar.

Luce gave her a hug, then pulled back and looked at her. "Have you been taking the supplements I gave you? You look pale."

Chris crossed her fingers and winked at Midge. "Of course I have. They probably take a while to work."

Luce nodded. "You're right. It does take time for them to infiltrate all your cells. Well, don't give up."

"I won't."

Midge smiled at her politely.

"I want you to meet my new friend. Midge, this is my best friend, Luce Lucerne."

Midge came around the bar to shake her hand.

Luce looked at her stilts. "You're a . . ."

"Midget," Midge finished for her. "Nice to meet you," she said, holding out her hand.

"She's also a brilliant pastry chef," Chris said.

"I see. How fortuitous for Amadeus, but what happened to the car?"

"The pastry chef, Shirley, beat the crap out of it with a rolling pin," Chris explained, swinging an imaginary rolling pin. "I suppose it works a lot like a baseball bat. Did an awful number on the car. The insurance company will probably have to total it. Amadeus was in tears."

"I imagine she was quite heartbroken," Luce said.

Bernadette came flying in. "I'm so sorry I'm late," she said to Luce. She was fiddling with her earplug and shoving her cell phone into her purse.

Chris looked at her watch. The play didn't start for an hour.

"I was supposed to pick Luce up."

"It's all right, B. I figured you got held up. I'll just leave the truck here."

"What the hell happened to the BMW?" B. asked.

"The pastry chef got busy with a rolling pin," Midge explained.

"You're a . . ."

"Midget," Chris, Midge and Luce said in unison.

"And what's this about you getting a citation for littering and going to court? I'm going with you. I did pre-law. This charge is absurd."

Chris smiled. Bernadette always blew in like a dirt devil in your living room. They were used to her. Chris could tell B. made Midge nervous. She had unruly dark curly hair that she attempted to change by altering hairstyles every few months. Her voluptuous breasts were usually accented in revealing yet tasteful business suits. Tonight it was a dark brown one with an amber silk blouse. Chris rated her figure somewhere between Dolly Parton and Pamela Anderson.

"You don't have do that, B."

"I want to," B. insisted.

Bernadette was a one-woman overhaul show. She made multitasking look like child's play. The woman could do circles around the best of them, Chris mused.

"Before I went into real estate I toyed with becoming a lawyer. I think I would have made a damn good one."

"You're a Realtor?" Midge inquired.

"Yes, Bernadette Chavez Maestas at your service. You can call me B. for short." She pulled out a card from her breast pocket and handed it to Midge. "Are you selling a house?"

"No, I need to buy one."

"You're staying," Chris said, happy at the prospect.

"I think so. There's nothing for me in Dallas."

"That's awesome, Midge." Chris gave her an exuberant hug, causing Midge to spill her glass of water. "Sorry."

B. gave her a disapproving look as if to say, "We need to talk business here." "So what are you in the market for? Of course, we'll need to set you up with a mortgage broker. No hidden credit problems I need to know about?" B. stared intently at Midge as if her credit score would miraculously appear on her forehead.

"B., Midge's real name is Sarah Roswell," Chris said. She waited for the nickels to fall. It never took B. long.

"Roswell . . . pastry . . . Roswellian Puff Pastries. You're a—"

"Rich midget," Chris and Midge said in unison and then laughed hysterically.

"Fantastic!" B. said.

Luce rolled her eyes. "She's mono-focused on real estate," she told Midge.

"Which makes for a great Realtor," Chris said. She was glad

Midge was staying. She'd grown rather attached to their happy-hour meetings over the last two weeks. "Why don't you two have a cocktail while I help Midge finish and then we'll go. We still have plenty of time to get downtown and park. The play doesn't start for another forty-five minutes."

"Sounds good. Luce can catch me up on what everyone's been doing. Now, don't forget to call me, and I'll get you all set up, Midge."

"I won't."

B. and Luce sat at the bar and ordered drinks.

"Wow," Midge said when they got back to the kitchen.

"You get used to her."

"What are you ladies up to tonight?"

"We're going to see the *Vagina Monologues*. We like to keep Luce busy on this night. It's the night Claire died."

Midge nodded.

"You know, we could hang out sometimes. I mean especially since you're going to stay," Chris said, stacking the dishes in the dishwasher and not looking at her.

Midge touched her hand. "I like you too, Chris."

Chris have her a hug.

"Now go play with your friends."

Chapter Three

"I'll be right there," Chris yelled out the front door. She took a quick look in the hall mirror, fixed an errant strand of hair and flew out the door.

Bernadette was waiting in her pearl-colored, leather-seated Lexus sedan to take her to court. Luce had gone shopping with Chris and found her a tasteful outfit in a fancy consignment store in Nob Hill. It was a tailored dark green suit with a beige dress shirt that was lightly embroidered on the front with sage thread. Luce told her she didn't want to look like a woman who littered on a regular basis and proceeded to select an expensive pair of leather shoes for her.

Chris got in the car. B. was studying the front of Chris's one-story adobe house with its small veranda on the front. The front yard was xeriscaped, so it required virtually no maintenance. "No maintenance" described her whole house. She could tell as

B. looked at it that she was going to get the you-should-trade-up sales talk. Before B. could start, Chris said, "I like my house."

B. chuckled. "You know me too well."

"We've been friends for fifteen years."

"But isn't it a little small?" B. asked as she pulled away from the curb and started down the street.

"No, it's just perfect. Have I grown? There's still only me and I'm still five foot five, one hundred and twenty pounds."

"Is that all you weigh? That's disgusting. I weighed that much when I was twelve."

"You have other accoutrements."

"What about your girlfriends?" B. was not to be deterred.

"They don't live with me. They just kind of stay." She noticed B. was dressed in a smart camel's-hair suit with a white silk blouse. Chris peered down at her shoes. They looked like a dark brown version of those square-heeled Puritan shoes, complete with a gold buckle. It was a good thing she wore a uniform to work because she'd never get this dress-up act. Each day after she took off her blue shorts and polo with the postal emblem she put on jeans and a T-shirt or shorts if it was warm. It was simple.

"You might meet someone someday who you want to permanently move in and then you'll need a bigger house. Interest rates are low right now." B. maneuvered the car through a variety of side streets until they came to Central, which they'd take downtown to the courthouse. B. knew the city better than anyone.

"This one's paid for, remember? Blood-money house."

B. winced. They had all been friends with Claire. Her untimely death had affected them deeply. Chris wondered how many years would have to pass before the mention of her name didn't dredge up unpleasant memories.

"Do you have to call it that?"

"It's true. She gave me the money because she felt guilty."

"And because Luce insisted. I don't know why you two didn't get together. You and Luce would have made a much better couple."

"Because, as you well know, Claire got there first and she wouldn't even allow us to be friends." Chris watched as the buildings of downtown came into view. If she hadn't been so nervous she would have been terribly annoyed with B. for bringing the whole thing up.

"Oh, that's right. You two were clandestine friends."

"Whatever. Are you sure you're up to this?"

"Up to what?" B. flicked on her turn indicator and drove into the parking garage of the municipal courthouse.

"Getting me off my littering charge."

"Of course. Once I explain your psychological situation at the time of the incident, I'm sure it will be thrown out of court. You look very nice, by the way." B. parked the car. She looked Chris over again as if to confirm her earlier judgment.

"Luce picked it out for me."

"She has good taste." B. grabbed a manila folder from the backseat.

Chris's eyes got wide and her stomach did a somersault. "What's that?"

"It's your legal brief."

Chris had had some trepidation about letting B. help her with this. Now she was contemplating risking a warrant for her arrest by not showing up for court. "My legal brief? B., this is a littering charge, not a murder trial."

"Exactly, and once I explain that to the judge she'll see how ludicrous this whole thing is."

They got out of the car. Chris was not reassured. They went through the weapons' scanners, no problem. B.'s heels made sharp noises on the hard marble tiles. She turned off her cell phone as the guard had instructed her. She kept flipping open her folder and looking at her notes as if she were mentally preparing her argument. Chris's palms began to sweat. She had a bad feeling about this.

Chris was hoping they wouldn't be called first so she'd have a chance to sum up the judge. As a mailman she had seventeen years of studying people's habits and mannerisms. Like a good shrink she could tell a lot about a person by careful observation.

The presiding judge was the Honorable Mary Baca. Everyone rose when she entered the room and made her way to the bench. A sturdy woman with short gray hair and dark-rimmed glasses, she climbed into her chair, which must have had a phone book on the seat, because she was rather short. She reminded Chris of the orange-haired midgets in the funny white pants in Willy Wonka's chocolate factory.

She didn't get her wish. Her name was called first. B. hopped up in eager anticipation of the forthcoming battle. Chris knew for certain this was going to turn out badly. She could feel it.

"Are you Chris McCoy?" The judge seemed confused by the two of them standing side by side.

"No, I'm her representation. Bernadette Chavez Maestas," B. said, straightening out her blazer.

The judge looked down at her paperwork. "For a littering charge?"

"Yes."

"Are you a lawyer?"

"Not exactly. I'm a Realtor."

"A Realtor?" Judge Baca raised her eyebrows.

"I'm fully prepared. I did pre-law at U of N.M."

"Ms. McCoy, are you comfortable with this?"

Chris felt like God On High had come down to question her. If she gave the incorrect answer there would be dire consequences. If she betrayed B. she'd lose one of her best friends. B. had seen her through tough times and she'd give her the shirt off her back—even if it was dry-clean-only. But letting B. represent her meant she could be on litter patrol for the rest of her life. She gave B. a quick smile. Picking up trash for fifty years wouldn't be that bad. "I trust her with my life."

B. gave her a squeeze. "Don't worry. I'll take care of you."

Chris refrained from saying, "That's what I'm afraid of."

"Proceed," Judge Baca said. She looked at Chris dubiously.

"On the day in question, the defendant had a traumatic experience and she wasn't thinking straight. It was at that moment that the littering occurred."

"You're trying to get your client off on an insanity plea for littering?" Judge Baca said.

"Precisely," B. said. She began to cite other cases where criminals had gotten off because they were crazy.

The judge interrupted her. "Ms. Maestas, I don't think any of your massive research applies here. Ms. McCoy, why don't you explain to me why you were temporarily littering."

"Well, you see, my—I mean, the person I was involved with had taken this stupid compatibility test—"

B. interjected. "I don't see how delving into Ms. McCoy's personal affairs is relevant here."

"It is if it explains her behavior."

"I beg to differ. You know she's a lesbian and you're going to make her stand up here and air her dirty laundry just because she's gay."

"That thought never crossed my mind, and once again, if I may reiterate, Ms. McCoy's sexual orientation has nothing whatsoever to do with her misdemeanor charge." Judge Baca's face turned red.

"I beg to differ once again. Her girlfriend was banging her climbing instructor in Chris's bed. She then gives her some lame excuse about a magazine personality test that Chris rips up in front of a cop. Her being gay has everything to do with it."

Chris put her head down on the table in mortification. She'd be picking up trash until the end of time.

"Ms. Maestas, you will refrain from using sexually explicit terms in my courtroom."

"Since when is *banging* a sexually explicit term? *Cunnilingus*, on the other hand—"

"That does it. One more word out of you and I'll hold you in contempt of court and you'll be spending the night in jail."

"You can't do that!" B.'s face was as red as the judge's.

"Bailiff, take Ms. Maestas and book her for contempt. Ms. McCoy, given the circumstances, I think you've been sufficiently punished. I grant you a suspended sentence. Don't litter anymore."

"I won't. Thank you," Chris said.

B. was about to say something when Chris clamped her hand over her mouth and whispered, "Don't say another word or you'll be spending the next month in jail. Give me the car keys. I'll explain this to Diane and pick you up in the morning. Got it?"

B. nodded. She glared at the judge as the bailiff came toward her. Judge Baca sat watching. "Ms. Maestas, a word of advice. I recommend you stick to real estate."

Chris thought B. was going to blow out of her skin. Luckily, just then a huge hailstorm erupted, the kind they got in May when the weather went wacky a few more times before it settled into the calm blue skies of June and July only to be interrupted by the monsoons of August. Nothing could be heard over the racket, so B.'s sputtering went unnoticed.

"Be good," Chris said.

B. scowled at the judge and let the bailiff escort her out of the courtroom.

Chris was in the parking garage when her cell phone went off. It was B. "What are you doing?"

"I get one call. I can't believe this. I'm going to check into this judge."

"B., be careful. I'll never forgive myself if something happens to you in there."

"Sweetheart, you forget, I'm a South Valley girl. I know how to act. Beneath this polished exterior is a lion cub. I'll just pretend I'm a call girl who got suckered."

"Great. Well, don't overdo it."

"But I need you to kind of smooth this over with Diane. She's been a little miffed at me lately."

"I'm going over there right now." Chris poked the nose of the Lexus out of the parking structure. She wanted to make sure the hail had stopped.

"Don't worry. I have a plan to fix it."

"That's what scares me." Chris turned onto Central.

"Oh, ye of little faith. Well, it appears I have to go."

Chris could imagine the bailiff indicating her two minutes were up and B. treating him like a pesky underling. She made the light and headed toward Diane and B.'s Northeast Heights home.

Chapter Four

When Chris pulled up in front of the house, Diane was attempting to cover a pile of furniture in the front yard with a large blue tarp. The hailstorm had turned to drizzle.

Chris jumped out of the car. "Here, let me help you." She grabbed the other end of the tarp.

"Thanks," Diane said.

Chris noticed she'd been crying. Her face was puffy and her eyes were red. "B. didn't tell me you guys were having a garage sale." The wind had caught the tarp again and Chris grabbed it.

"We're not. This is her stuff. I'm throwing her out."

"What?"

Diane tied the rope around B.'s leather armchair. "Where is she?"

"She's in jail." Chris tied her end of the tarp to a red toolbox. "I thought you were the one in trouble."

"I was. I got a suspended sentence but B. got cited with contempt of court."

"Let me guess. She couldn't keep her big mouth shut."

Chris nodded. "She has to spend the night in jail."

"That's perfect. She can't even show up for the grand finale of our relationship."

"I'm sure she'd like to be here, but you know, the incarceration thing."

The drizzle had turned to rain and the tarp was whipping around again.

"I give up," Diane said, throwing her arms up in the air. "Tell her to come get her stuff."

"Diane, wait. Can't we talk about this?"

"What's there to talk about? Look, I know B.'s your friend, but she doesn't make a good partner. Remember how you jumped out of the car to help me with the tarp?"

"Yeah." Chris hated leading questions. They always got her in trouble.

"B. would have waved at me on her way into the house because she was making some big deal on her cell phone. There's more to life than money. I need someone who is really here, not off somewhere in real-estate-mega-million land."

"I understand. I'll take her stuff to my house."

"Thank you."

Chris watched as Diane went back inside. She was a pretty brunette, with a petite figure, brown almost black eyes and a turned-up nose. The kind of face you could trust. The kind of woman who'd love you forever. Chris had to admit that B. fucked up. Not to mention Jordan, Diane's six-year-old daughter, who adored B.

She called Luce. "We have a situation here. You've got to bring your truck to B.'s. Diane threw her out and B.'s in jail."

"Oh, no. I'll be right there."

That was one of the things Chris liked about Luce. She took

crises in stride. She didn't ask a zillion questions. She did what needed to be done. Chris wished she could find a girlfriend with one tenth of Luce's common sense.

She secured the tarp as best she could and waited in the car for Luce. The storm subsided. In the summer the high and low fronts often collided and created freaky storms. She was an avid weather-watcher, partly because she worked outside and partly because her main mode of transportation was a motorcycle. She hated the storms. They were a biker's nightmare—wet streets meant puddles and loss of traction, and at fifty miles an hour rain felt like rubber bullets slamming against your skin.

When Luce pulled up in the driveway, Chris's stress factor dropped down several notches. Luce handled things so much better. Perhaps she could talk some sense into Diane. They could put B.'s stuff back in the house and no one would know. Chris got out of the car.

Luce gave her a hug. "How much jail time did you get?"

"I got a suspended sentence. The judge felt sorry for me having B. as my lawyer. B. got a night in jail for contempt of court. She couldn't keep her trap shut."

Luce laughed. "Well, I guess there is a silver lining in all of this."

"A silver lining?" Chris said. "This is my fault."

Then sun popped through the clouds and seemed to shine directly on B.'s pile of possessions. Chris hoped it wasn't Godspeak.

"No, it's not. This was a long time coming. Let me talk to Diane. Load the small things and I'll help with the recliner."

"Maybe you can fix it."

"In light of the circumstances, I'd say that's wishful thinking," Luce said, pointing at the pile of stuff. "I don't think Diane went to all this trouble to change her mind. Besides, it looked like she had help."

Chris hadn't thought of that. Was there another woman? Chris nodded in defeat. She loaded boxes in the back of Luce's beat-up white Dodge truck. Luce used it mainly to haul small supplies. For the big stuff, like huge pieces of glass, she used a delivery service. Claire hated that truck and was forever begging Luce to get a new one because it embarrassed her. Luce didn't care. Chris admired her for that—she didn't bother about others' opinions. B. could take a lesson from Luce. B. spent a lot of time crafting the right image. Sometimes Chris wondered if the real B. was still in there. Perhaps that's what Diane was going on about. She scratched her head, looking at the house, the half-full truck and the ruination of her friend's life.

Luce came out of the house. "Will the recliner fit?"

"Yes, I saved room at the back. We'll have to turn it upside down."

They each grabbed a side and hoisted it into the truck.

"I guess that's it then. Just another relationship down the toilet," Chris said. She kept looking at the house, hoping Diane would come rushing out with a change of heart.

"Chris, she's angry. B.'s not always the best partner. She's a great provider but she's self-absorbed. She's a little too focused on what B. wants and tends to ignore the rest."

"Is that what Diane said?"

"Verbatim."

"Great. Here, you get the back and I'll get the front and we'll put the tarp over everything." Chris said. Looking like the Beverly Hillbillies, they pulled away from the house.

"Where are we taking it?" Luce asked.

They both started to laugh. "This isn't funny," Chris said, wiping her eyes.

"It is, kind of. Think about it. B. is incarcerated and can't do anything. All her beloved worldly possessions are piled high in a beat-up pickup truck, and we're trying to figure out where she's going to live. It's poetic justice."

"Fuck, this isn't going to be pretty."

"She can stay at my house."

"Too far out. The commute would drive her nuts. She can

stay at my place. I've got the spare room and she can use my office. That'll make it more tolerable."

"You're so sweet."

"Don't let that get around."

Luce got on the freeway and headed toward Carlyle Street and Chris's house. The clouds had cleared and a perfect blue sky had taken their place as if the storm had never happened. *Wouldn't it be nice if parts of your life could do that?* Chris thought as she watched the blue tarp billow behind them in the bed of the truck.

They moved B.'s boxes into the garage and put her flat-screen television on the cherry wood entertainment center where Chris's had been. They barely got B.'s leather recliner through the front door. After several attempts at rearranging the living room furniture they came up with something that worked. B.'s and Chris's recliners sat side by side.

"Oh, how sweet, two old maids with their dueling easy chairs," Chris said.

"Stop it. Neither of you are old maids."

Chris flounced down in her chair. It was leather as well but didn't look nearly so nice as B.'s. "What the fuck is going on?"

Luce sat in B.'s. She discovered the massage feature. "Wow, this is nice."

"Only the best for B."

"What do mean what's going on?"

"It's like an epidemic. First me, then Amadeus and now B. and Diane."

"Yours was trivial, Amadeus's was a fling and B.'s was a tragedy that could have been avoided had she been more attentive." Luce played with the controls and now had herself prone in the chair. She looked over at Chris. "How do I get back up?"

"I don't know, but you'd better be careful. Knowing B. this thing collapses into a neat briefcase and if you press the wrong button you could end up inside."

They both laughed.

"Will you go with me to pick up B. tomorrow?" Chris asked.

"Don't you have to work?"

"I called in for emergency annual. B. is going to need some moral support."

"Is annual like your vacation time and sometimes you can use it in an emergency?"

Chris laughed. "I forget not everyone works for the government. Yes. We accrue eight hours per pay period that can be used throughout the year for vacations or spot days off or in an emergency."

"Wow, that's flexible."

"So will you come?"

"Of course. As a self-employed person, I can take any day off."

"Thanks. I owe you. We'll grill a couple of rib eyes and have some beers and maybe we can come up with a creative way to tell B. her world just got turned upside down."

"It might not be that bad."

Chris rolled her eyes. She got up and peered at the controls on B.'s chair. Luce's face had turned red. Chris managed to get her upright but lifted the footrest as well so now Luce looked like the letter V.

"Perhaps we should sit out back on my simple wooden chairs that don't have controls."

"Great idea," Luce said, taking Chris's hand so she could get out of the chair.

Twilight was setting in. Chris lit her torches and started the gas grill. She got them both a beer.

Luce leaned back in her chair and closed her eyes. She let out a heavy sigh. "This is so much better."

"Simplicity has its merits." Chris chugged her beer and knew why alcohol had been invented.

Chapter Five

"I'm telling you the market is hot. Three of you bundle your resources together, buy a house, fix it up, sell it and you're on your way to financial freedom," B. told a group of six scantily clad women in stiletto heels.

Only B. would be giving a real-estate seminar to a group of prostitutes in the booking area of the county jail, Chris thought as she and Luce waited for her.

B. waved at them. "Hi, girls. I'll be right there."

Chris smiled back. She was glad Luce was with her. Luce had ended up spending the night instead of driving out to Placitas. Earlier that morning she'd made Chris stop pacing as she practiced her speech to B.

B. was ecstatic to see them. She hugged them as if she'd been away for months. "Luce, you didn't have to come."

"I wanted to give you moral support," Luce replied, giving Chris a look.

"Oh, I'm fine. How did Diane take it? You know she hates these little snafus of mine."

"Well, we kind of got another little snafu," Chris said.

"She's mad. I'll stop and get her some flowers. Maybe a bracelet. I saw the cutest mother-of-pearl one just the other day."

"Uh, B., it's more complicated than that. See, we couldn't call you while you were in the clink so we had to make some decisions on our own."

B. stared at Chris hard and then looked at Luce. "What the hell is she talking about?"

"Diane threw you out yesterday and we moved you in with Chris."

"What! I'm going to talk to her. This is completely unacceptable."

Chris was exhibiting her usual behavior in a crisis. She was going to call a cab and go to a hotel and stay there until this whole thing blew over.

Luckily, Luce took charge. She put her hands firmly on B.'s shoulders and looked her right in the eye. "Diane told me that if you go anywhere near the house or Jordan she'll slap a restraining order on you and you'll never get visitation."

"I see."

Chris watched as B. registered that her world had collapsed. She waited until she was in the backseat of her Lexus to sob and wail. Chris thanked God for this.

Over the hullabaloo in the back, Chris suggested they get breakfast at the Zoo and then take B. to Chris's.

"Food always takes her mind off her troubles," Chris told Luce as they pulled out of the parking garage.

"Great! Then I'll be fat and no one will want me," B. blubbered.

"Is this like the road to perdition?" Chris asked.

"No, it's longer," Luce replied.

They got B. inside after they dried her face and straightened out her crumpled suit. Amadeus and Midge were waiting for them. Midge came over and patted B.'s shoulder. She was dressed in her kitchen garb.

"I made you a special pastry to raise your spirits," Midge said, pushing a plateful toward B.

"Thanks, Midge." B. looked at it morosely.

"So it appears your gluttonous pursuit of money has cost you your family. Good going," Amadeus said.

B. started to cry again. What was left of her mascara ran down her face.

"You're really helping the situation. We just got her stopped," Chris said, grabbing a handful of cocktail napkins and giving them to B.

"How does everyone know already?" B. asked. She blew her nose and looked pitiful.

"Diane put up a billboard on the freeway," Amadeus replied.

This produced a fresh torrent of tears.

"What is it with you Germans? Why don't you get a filet knife and cut out her heart and then sprinkle the wound with pickling salt," Chris said. She patted B.'s shoulder.

"B., I was only kidding. Diane came by last night for a talk. She's upset as well," Amadeus said.

"She's not a displaced person at least," B. replied.

"No, but she does have a child to explain this to," Amadeus replied.

More blubbering ensued.

"Sweet Jesus, Amadeus, shut your trap," Chris said, shoving more napkins at B.

"She's only trying to help," Luce said.

"I'm simply stating the obvious," Amadeus said, glaring at Chris.

"Perhaps, if it's all right with Chris, we could have a barbeque and help B. with her transition," Luce suggested.

Amadeus nodded. "Now, that sounds practical."

"All right, dinner at seven at blood-money house," Chris said.

"We got some fresh salmon in this morning. I'll bring that," Amadeus said.

"I'll hit the farmer's market and get some salad stuff," Luce said.

"Midge, are you available?" Chris asked shyly.

"Of course. I'll bring dessert."

B.'s mood brightened. "It will keep my mind off it."

"Great, we'll meet at seven," Chris said, suddenly wondering how much cleaning she was going to have to do.

Amadeus went in the back and brought out their order, three plates of eggs Benedict. "The hollandaise sauce is perfect."

"Chris won't let me get fat," B. said with apparent trepidation as she snatched a pastry.

"Wal-Mart has stationary bikes on sale for forty-nine bucks. We'll get two and ride on the back patio," Chris said as she attacked her eggs with a fervor. She got more than enough exercise at work but to keep B. happy she'd do anything.

"We could join a gym," B. said.

"Just not the one with the rock-climbing wall," Chris said, remembering the old wound.

"You should try mine. It's women only," Amadeus said.

Chris envisioned amazons pumping massive amounts of iron and a Soviet-style woman in uniform ordering, "More, more, more." They'd eat B. alive. Stationary bicycles—B. could make calls while she pedaled her way to a slimmer trimmer figure. B. had finished her breakfast and was licking hollandaise sauce off her fingers. Chris was going to say something when Luce gave her the please-be-kind look.

"You know, that gives me an idea," Chris said.

"And what might that be?" Luce asked.

"I'll tell you tonight," Chris replied.

They left the restaurant. B. didn't cry all the way home. Chris was relieved.

39

She made some coffee while B. took several phone calls from prospective clients. *At least if she's busy she'll get over the bumpy first couple of days*, Chris thought. Not that her liaisons counted like the five years B. had spent with Diane, although the seven years she'd been with Claire did. It hurt when it ended. Every morning she thought she was going to die and every night she cried herself to sleep. Time was endless, and then one day she caught a woman cruising her at the gym. They'd gone to bed that afternoon and suddenly Claire hadn't mattered so much.

That's what B. needed, what Amadeus needed and what Luce needed. They would start a dating club to find the perfect mate for each of them. Instead of letting love fall to chance, they would research it, explore all the places where it might lurk or frolic and nail it to the wall of each of their futures. This meant no bars, coworkers, blind dates or setups from well-meaning friends. This was a quest.

She looked over at Luce, who was studying her large bed of orange daylilies that grew around the koi pond. Her landscaper had insisted that every yard needed a pond. Chris thought the whole thing was overrated. The fish kept breeding and Chris had to find homes for them. "Want some fish?"

"Are they overpopulating again?" Luce said. She sipped her coffee and studied the daylilies again.

"I have to go," B. said, suddenly clicking off the phone and glancing at Chris and Luce. "But I'll be back by two to help with the arrangements and the cleaning." She eyed Chris. B. was a meticulous housekeeper. Chris was going to have to bone up. Living alone was definitely easier. She'd start by putting away the laundry piled high on the living room couch.

"All right then," Chris said.

Luce helped her clear away the coffee mugs. She kissed her on the cheek. "I've got some work to do."

"Thanks for helping out."

❧

Everyone showed promptly at seven. B. had straightened out Chris's house with the efficacy of a team of Merry Maids. Chris took an hour-long nap after it was done while B. put the Tupperware drawer in order. Chris was now sprinkling dill and squeezing lemon juice on the salmon before putting it on the barbeque. Amadeus kept a watchful eye. When Chris was finished she carried the salmon outside. Amadeus followed. The others were already lounging about the back veranda.

"So what's your idea?" she prodded.

"Has it been bothering you?" Chris asked. Tormenting Amadeus was high on her list of sadistic pleasantries.

"Not at all. Just curious."

"I'd like to know," Luce said. She sipped her glass of Merlot.

B. was sitting in the chaise lounge leafing through her brokers' magazine and muttering something about the broker of the month on the cover. Keeping busy all afternoon was helpful but Chris could tell morbidity had slipped in the back door now that things had slowed down. B. turned the pages savagely. "I like plans. Then I know how to function. Spill it, girl."

"I think we should start a Date Night Club," Chris said. She took a key-lime martini from the tray Midge was holding. "Thank you."

"Hmm," Amadeus replied, obviously not impressed with her idea. She peered at the salmon, resting beside the grill.

"Don't worry, I'm turning the cooking over to you," Chris said, handing her the stainless steel fork. Amadeus nodded. She put the fish on the grill.

"Date Night Club? What on earth is that?" B. put the magazine down with a slap.

Luce had squatted down and was acutely studying the orange daylilies again.

"You can take some of those home," Chris said. She suspected Luce was mentally arranging them into one of her stained-glass pieces. Luce's work was akin to Georgia O'Keefe's flowers in terms of size but the glass work gave them a different luminance.

"Earth calling Chris," B. said. "Explanation."

"Oh, well, what I thought was that one night a week we would all go out and try to find Ms. Right."

"What, like at a bar?" B. said.

"No, I was thinking something more creative."

"As in?" Amadeus said. She flipped the salmon to sear the other side and closed the lid on the grill, carefully checking the vents. Obviously satisfied, she turned her full attention to Chris.

"It appears that we all have certain patterns we need to break."

Midge sat in a chair under the umbrella and sipped her martini. "Yes. For example, I like short women."

Chris sat down next to her. They started to giggle and then laugh, slapping their knees. The others looked on, evidently puzzled by the joke. Midge told her once over martinis that it was fun to make jokes about herself and that one of the hardest things about being a midget was that everyone tried to ignore the fact. She was a midget. Small jokes were funny and it was all right to laugh. So far Chris was the only one who got it.

"Midge, I think in your case, someone's height is a relative concern," Amadeus said.

"I would like someone more my size," Midge said. "I realize that cuts down my options."

"We're questing for Ms. Right, the ultimate partner," Chris said, getting caught up in her own fervor. "This isn't about booty. It's about true love."

"Is there such a thing?" B. said, getting teary.

"Yes," Chris said emphatically. She wasn't well qualified to speak on the subject but like any good evangelical speaker she could deliver the message and enthuse the follower. That, she knew was one of her strengths.

"You said we all have patterns. What do you think is my pattern?" Amadeus sipped her wine and sat down. She chose a barstool near the grill. She crossed her legs and looked mildly amused.

This was a loaded question. Chris smiled sweetly and replied, "We both have the same pattern. Two birds, one stone. Does 'flaky nymphomaniacs' ring any bells?"

Amadeus smiled. "I vote you president of the club."

"Thank you."

"What about mine?" B. asked.

"No women with children. You want kids, have your own so no one can take them away." Chris waited for the explosion.

Instead, B. was quiet for a moment. "You're absolutely right!" She pursed her lips and nodded as if imbibing this concept for the first time.

Luce looked relieved.

"And you," Chris said, pointing at Luce, "no more moody artists. You need someone who'll make you laugh."

"What exactly are you looking for?" Luce asked.

"Someone sane. Someone so natural and uninhibited she makes love with her socks on because she has cold feet. That's what I want."

Luce laughed. "Well, that narrows it down."

"And someone who doesn't cheat," Chris added.

"I'm in," Amadeus said. She lifted the lid on the grill. "I think we're close."

"Good. I'm starving," B. said. She eyed Chris. "I can be hungry. We rode those stupid bikes for forty minutes."

"We did," Chris said, looking at the two white gym towels hanging over the handlebars of the stationary bikes they'd bought at Wal-Mart.

Amadeus got a serving platter and carefully put the salmon on it. Luce pulled the spinach and watercress salad from the fridge while Chris and Midge set the patio table. Midge brought out her puff pastry. Luce opened a bottle of Pinot Noir and Chris looked on enviously. She sucked at opening wine. Despite her occasional successes, Luce only let her do it when they were alone because she usually busted the cork. She did the same thing with scrambled eggs.

"I want to propose a toast." Luce held up her glass. "To Date Night Club and finding the perfect girl."

"Hear, hear," Amadeus, B. and Chris said.

Midge smiled. "Yes, to the perfect girl."

Amadeus cut the salmon into portions and expertly served them. She had foil-wrapped small red potatoes seasoned with garlic cloves and parsley. Now she unwrapped them into a serving bowl and passed it around.

"This is absolutely marvelous," Midge said.

"The salmon was flown in this morning. Fish has to be fresh," Amadeus said.

Chris studied Amadeus's stunning profile. With her wavy red hair, the deepest blue eyes she'd ever seen and a long lean body with muscles in all the right places, she was a catch. A woman like that should have an equally stunning partner, she thought. This was not the case. In the six years Chris had known her there'd been no one steady. Amadeus's track record closely resembled her own.

B. put a huge helping of red potatoes on her plate. She avoided Chris's reprising gaze. "I'll go for a walk on my lunch hour."

"Amadeus, did you ever have one great love?" Chris inquired. Her curiosity had gotten the better of her.

Amadeus arched an eyebrow. "Why do you ask?" She took a bite of salmon and gave her an impenetrable stare.

"You know, answering a question with a question is considered an evasive tactic often used when one is avoiding a subject," Chris replied. Amadeus would've made a great politician or a professional poker player.

Amadeus conceded. "I will not be alone in my confession."

"I'll go next," Midge said. She took a drink of wine and waited for Amadeus to speak.

"All right. She was my first love and I botched it. I started my first restaurant. This was in Berlin. She was there helping and nurturing me. She was so supportive. She wanted me to achieve my dream even more than I did. Once the restaurant started to get noticed so did I. I fell hard. I thought I could have her and also the others that wanted me. I broke her heart." Amadeus was pensive. She took a sip of wine and continued. "We parted. I sold the restaurant and came here. I needed the farthest place on the planet. No one in Germany knows of New Mexico."

"How'd she find out?" Chris asked. She poured everyone more wine whether they needed it or not. Perhaps Midge was right. If they got their hurts out in the open maybe each of them could get on with finding someone substantial.

"There was this hotel across from the restaurant. I rented a room there. Sometimes I would work so late it was just easier to stay there. My beloved understood this. She didn't want me driving home exhausted. I might crash. She was that devoted to me." Amadeus sat back in her chair and stared off into space.

Chris could only imagine the horrors that were running through Amadeus's head. They waited. That was one positive attribute about being single lesbians, Chris thought. It made them empathetic.

"She found me with two Spanish women in the hotel room."

"Wow, that must have been quite a sight," B. said, savagely forking her salmon.

Luce touched Amadeus's shoulder. B.'s first girlfriend had been a notorious philanderer. Chris had warned her but B. was so wrapped up in the newness of woman-love that she barreled through all the red flags like a race horse foaming and sweating for the finish line. She came home early from a business trip and found her girlfriend in the pool fucking another woman.

"B., could you pass the salad," Chris said, noticing that Midge had been waiting for it patiently.

"Sure," B. said, thrusting it at Midge.

"B., take it easy," Luce said.

"I'm sorry. Everytime the cheating thing comes up I get

45

stressed out. I should have cut out Vanessa's clitoris right then and there."

Chris winced.

"You should have known better. That woman had slept with half the lesbians in town. It's not like we didn't warn you," Amadeus replied.

B. slugged down the rest of her wine. "It's not like my track record has improved." She started to sniffle.

Midge stroked her hand. "It makes it harder when the relationship was long. I was in love with a straight woman for years. We never had sex but I loved her with all my heart. Then one day she told me she was getting married. I thought I was going to die."

"You never had sex?" Chris said, horrified by the very thought.

Amadeus took a bite of salmon and furrowed her brow at Chris, indicating she was out of line.

"I mean, platonic relationships have their place," Chris said.

Amadeus nodded at her approvingly.

"I'm never going to have sex again. I'll end up a fat, lonely lesbian," B. said, gesturing for more salmon.

"Why do you keep talking about getting fat?" Luce asked, handing her the platter.

"She's gained a couple pounds since last week," Chris replied. "Nothing a little exercise won't cure."

"But she only got thrown out yesterday," Luce said.

Chris shrugged.

"Imagine what's going to happen by next week," B. said, putting two thick filets of salmon on her plate.

Chris reached over and took one of the pieces. "I won't let you get fat. I'll duct-tape your mouth shut if I have to."

As B. started to blubber again, her cell phone rang. She picked it up and immediately flipped into Realtor mode. "I'm fine. It's my allergies. Now about that asking price . . ."

The rest of the conversation was a series of real-estate terms that interested no one. Chris wondered if B. picked up her cell phone when she was making love. Perhaps Diane had experienced coitus interruptus one too many times. B. always answered her phone. It didn't matter if she was in the middle of a dinner party or the middle of a crisis. She loved blathering on about houses.

B. clicked off. "Now, where were we?" she said, dabbing her running mascara with the corner of her napkin.

Chris grabbed B.'s cell phone. "Did it ever occur to you that this might be part of your problem?" She switched the phone off.

"What are you doing?" B. asked. She squirmed uncomfortably in her chair.

"You're addicted to this phone," Chris replied.

"No, I'm not!" B. attempted to grab it back.

"Then sit still with it turned off," Chris said.

Everyone watched the battle of wills.

"Fine," B. said finally.

"Great." Chris kept her eye on her.

Suddenly B. lunged for the phone. It went flying out of Chris's hand, flipped up in the air and landed with a plop in the small fish pond located directly behind Chris not far from the daylilies.

"Oh, shit!" Chris got up and peered into the murky water.

B. watched the surface of the pond as if waiting for the phone to miraculously pop up, crying for Mommy. Chris grabbed a nearby net that she used to clean debris and the occasional dead fish out of the pond. Try as she might, she couldn't locate the phone.

"Just leave it," B. said. She squatted at the water's edge looking forlorn. "Maybe you're right. Diane used to get angry with me because I always had the phone plastered to my ear."

Luce patted her shoulder. Amadeus handed her a drink. It

was Midge who struck the final chord. "B., you're a really good Realtor. People will leave a message. You shouldn't worry so much."

"I know. I get scared sometimes," B. replied. Chris took her hand.

"Scared of what?" Luce asked as she squatted next to B. on the grass.

"Of being alone," she said, looking at her friends gathered round her.

"You're not alone. You have us," Luce said.

"And we've got Date Night Club," Chris added. "Now, remember the mission statement of our group. When you stand them on their heads they all look like sisters." She smiled mischievously. "The janitor at work gave me that piece of advice."

"That's disgusting," Amadeus said. She went to sit down on the patio. The others followed.

"I don't get it," B. said petulantly.

"The power of the triangle." Chris made a V with her thumbs and forefingers.

B. still looked confused. Luce whispered in B.'s ear. Chris watched as B. got it. "That's horrid," she said.

"But it's true. We're looking for quality here, not quantity," Chris replied.

"All right. Count me in," B. said, getting up. "But right now I have to go sell a house."

"Do you want to take my cell phone?" Chris offered.

"Oh, that won't be necessary. I have several spare ones." B. paused, looking contemplative. "I always seem to have technical issues, or they have a habit of going missing."

Chris gave Luce a knowing look. She could just imagine Diane doing bad things to B.'s cell phone.

After B. left, Amadeus and Midge stayed for dessert and coffee. Then they headed back to the restaurant.

Chris and Luce stood next to each other at the kitchen sink

washing the dishware that couldn't go in the dishwasher. Washing one of Luce's hand-carved teak salad bowls, she started to chuckle as she gazed out onto the pond.

"What?" Luce asked.

"B.'s phone in the pond."

They both started to laugh.

"I hope the koi don't figure out how to use it and start making long-distance phone calls," Chris said, "or I'm going to be in big trouble." Luce handed her the big white fish platter to wash. She liked spending time with Luce. She reminded herself to enjoy this time alone with her because if Date Night Club worked, Luce would have a girlfriend soon. She tried to imagine the kind of woman she would pick. She found it difficult—the only one she could think of was Claire, the only woman they had both loved.

Luce broke her musing. "What are you thinking about?"

Chris contemplated lying. "I was trying to figure out what kind of a woman each of us will fall in love with." She glanced up at Luce. Luce's hazel eyes met hers and for a moment neither she or Luce spoke.

"Good people, the right kind of people," Luce said resolutely, as if saying it aloud might make it come true.

"Damn, I hope you're right. I'm sick of fuck-ups."

Luce hung up the dish towel. "I better go. I need to get some stuff organized for tomorrow."

"I know. Thanks for getting us through this."

"Call me if B. starts getting fussy. I'll take her shopping and get her nails done. Pouring your life story out to a nail tech is very cathartic."

"I wouldn't know." Chris rolled her eyes.

"It's a girl thing," Luce said. She reached out for Chris.

Chris held her longer than was necessary. Luce never pulled away. Perhaps it was the closeness they'd been denied under Claire's watchful eye earlier in their friendship that allowed for this. Sometimes she would open the tiny box where she kept her feelings for Luce and let a little of its magic elixir spill out like expensive perfume. She'd dab a bit behind each ear and dream about a parallel universe where she and Luce were a couple instead of Luce and Claire. They would've made a good life, a sane life together. Instead, Claire found her first, screwed everything up and then vaporized. It was the story of Chris's life. She sighed and let Luce go.

Chapter Six

Chris groaned and rolled over. She looked at the clock, which read twelve thirty, and got out of bed. Dressed only in a sports bra and boxer shorts, she went to the living room. "B., what's wrong?" She rubbed her eyes, trying to concentrate on the current crisis.

B. was curled up in her leather easy chair, sobbing. Broken sounds came out that slightly resembled English.

Chris was forced to do some preliminary guesswork. "You didn't sell the house and that made you sad."

The sobbing grew louder.

"You sold the house but you got jacked on the commission?"

B. shook her head and seemed to calm down. The language of real estate always seemed to help her focus. "No, I sold the house and made a fortune." She blew her nose.

"Then what's wrong?"

"It doesn't matter anymore." She snatched another tissue from the box nestled on the arm of the chair.

Even when she was going to have a cry, B. was prepared, Chris thought wryly. "You've lost your zest for real estate." Truly alarmed, she shuddered at the thought. The mere idea of B. not having a focus gave her heart palpitations, especially since B. was under her care and guidance.

"Of course not," B. snapped. "It's just that usually when I had a big sale I'd buy something special for Jordan and now I can't." She started to blubber again, shoving her hand into the tissue box with such force she sent it flying.

Chris picked it up and handed it to her. "I know. Why don't you set up one of those college education funds for Jordan. Then you got her something special, only it's a secret."

B. stopped crying and looked at Chris like she was a genius.

"That's a brilliant idea. And very practical," B. said, wiping her eyes. "You're a good friend."

Chris let out a sigh of relief. How she pulled that out of her ass she'd never know. "We can get through this. Why don't we pull out the sleeper couch and watch a good old black-and-white movie until we fall asleep."

"All right. I'm having trouble sleeping lately," B. said sheepishly.

"I hadn't noticed."

B. got up and helped her unfold the bed. Chris found her copy of *Casablanca* and shoved the tape in the VCR. She turned around to find B. staring at her.

"I didn't know you had such a nice body."

"You've never seen me in my underwear before."

"You have a washboard stomach and well-defined arms," B. said, studying her physique.

Chris blushed. "Thanks, B." She went to the linen closet and got some bedding for the hideaway bed. She gave the sheets a good sniff. They smelled a little stale.

"I would never have known by the way you dress. All your clothes are so baggy. A good body is an asset. I think you should accentuate it more."

"B., in case you haven't noticed I'm a simple kind of gal."

B. was not to be assuaged. "I want to take you shopping and get you some real clothes."

"You don't have to do that, B. I'm fine, really." Chris threw the sheets on the bed. She didn't want to be the focus of B.'s new attentions.

"I'm living here. I want to do something nice for you. Please." B. smiled at her pleadingly as she helped make the bed.

Chris shrugged. "Sure, I'd love that."

"Great!" B. grabbed the remote and hopped onto the sofa bed. "This is going to be fun. Just like a slumber party."

Chris stifled a groan, thinking she was going to be exhausted tomorrow. She fluffed up her pillow and settled in.

The next morning Chris was standing in her supervisor's office. "Now, what happened?" She was dressed in a wrinkled blue polo shirt with a postal emblem and shorts. She didn't feel her best. The load of laundry that contained her work uniforms had sat in the dryer for two days and everything was horribly wadded up. She'd have to rewash them tonight. Taking care of B. was throwing off her schedule.

"Taylor got arrested for indecent exposure. One of his customers called the police when he knocked on her door buck naked except for his socks." Sid, her supervisor frowned.

Chris liked Sid. He was a short, slim Hispanic who always wore khaki Dockers and various shades of blue or green dress shirts. It was his uniform. He stroked his trimmed beard—a nervous habit that seemed to indicate he was thinking.

"His socks? What the hell was he doing? Did someone steal his clothes or something?"

"Not exactly. It appears he was jacking off and then went up to the door and told the woman who answered what he'd been up to."

"Has he lost his mind?"

"We did send him in for a psych evaluation."

Chris was the union steward for the station and it was her responsibility to make sure he got his job back. Not to mention that Taylor had a wife and three kids. She often wondered why she took this position. It was more headache than it was worth. This was one case she wasn't sure she could pull off. She was certain the union bylaws made no mention of removing all your clothes and spanking the monkey. "Why do you suppose he kept his socks on?"

"Toe jam?" Sid suggested.

They both started to laugh.

Sid wiped his eyes. "We got to get him back. He does a lot of overtime, and with a full roster of annual coming up we need him. With that many people on vacation we could be in serious trouble."

"Got any ideas?"

"I'll look for other incidents of like nature, and you be creative."

"Great."

"By the way, we got a new hire."

"That's good news," Chris said. She pulled on the front of her shirt, attempting to straighten out a particularly bad wrinkle.

Sid studied his clipboard with the day's assignments on it. He didn't meet her gaze. "The only OJI we have is Padilla and he's on annual. I was kind of hoping you could show her the ropes."

"Sid, my route backed up from being off, and you expect me to sub as an on-the-job instructor?" Chris said incredulously.

Sid pointed at the petite brunette standing beside Chris's workspace commonly referred to as one's case. She looked petrified. "We can't afford to lose another one. Kids these days. No fortitude," he said, shaking his head.

"All right, I'll do it. First-class letters and magazines only, and you get Cisco to put up the bulk mail while we're out delivering," Chris replied, knowing she had some leverage.

"You got it. Her name is Georgianna Lewis."

Chris stretched her neck to one side. It cracked. "I can't wait to meet her."

On the way to her case, Chris found herself on the outskirts of another postal crisis. Rodriguez was fighting with Chavez about a relay assignment.

"You're nothing but a fucking pussy. All you ever say is I can't do this, I can't do that. What can you do? You haven't got any balls," Rodriguez yelled.

"I've got more balls than you do," Chavez retorted.

"Yeah? Then why don't you prove it?"

Chavez dropped his shorts to reveal black knit boxers that resembled swimming trunks more than underwear. Chris silently thanked God he wasn't wearing briefs. She caught Georgianna staring at Chavez, her mouth agape. *It's no fucking wonder no one lasts here anymore*, she thought. *The inmates are running the asylum.*

"Oh, crap," she muttered. "Chavez, pull your pants up. We've already got one guy in trouble for exposing himself. We don't need another."

"I'm just showing it. I'm not spanking it." He pulled up his pants.

Someone let out a shrieking monkey call. Chris put her hands on her hips. "That's enough. We've got ladies present." She went to her case. "Come on, let's get you started." She dumped a tray of letters on the desktop in front of her. "I'm Chris, by the way."

Georgianna nodded. "So I really have to put all these letters in the little slots?" she said, her eyes wide as if the thought daunted her.

"Yes, each address has its own slot, but see, each street is color-coded. The numbers are odd on one side and even on the other depending on the line of travel. First, look at the number, then the street. Find the street on the case, then look for the number."

"What's the line of travel?"

"Each route starts in one place and ends somewhere else. We call it following the mail. The line of travel is the way that you go. You finish delivering one street and usually you turn right to find your next spot."

"Oh, I wondered how you knew where to go. It's like following a quadrant on a map."

"Exactly. Now let's find out what kind of a visual memory you have. Here, look at this magazine cover." Chris handed her a *Rolling Stone* magazine.

Georgianna looked at the cover. "It's Britney Spears."

"Let me demonstrate." Chris picked up a *Time* magazine with a picture of Chairman Mao on it—some retro look at communism, she supposed. She studied the cover and then handed the magazine over. She closed her eyes and then proceeded to describe the cover in detail—the yellow background, the rays of sun emanating from his head and the red border.

"Oh, I get it." Georgianna picked up a *Martha Stewart* magazine. The cover showed a white china cabinet and strawberries on a white linen tablecloth. Georgianna studied the cover, closed her eyes and described it perfectly to Chris.

"You'll make an excellent letter-carrier."

"Because I can describe magazine covers?"

"No, because you can memorize the position of streets on the case in the same way you visualized the cover." Chris pointed to the three metal boxes that made up her case. Each shelf had metal inserts that were comprised of an address, a color for each street and a name. "Now look at the case, visualize the position of the case and then close your eyes for a minute until you can see in your head where it's located on the shelf."

Georgianna followed her instructions. She picked up a handful of letters and started to case. "I think I get it." Her eyes sparkled with confidence.

"You can do this," Chris said. She squatted down and began sorting out mail, separating the bulk mail from the magazines and dividing them into different plastic tubs. She watched as Georgianna grew more sure of her ability. Her shoulders had straightened and her pace had picked up.

She could only be in her mid-twenties, Chris thought. She had been her age when she started with the post office. She looked around with a new sense of awareness at the things that had grown familiar over the years—carts of parcels, trays packed with letters, the clerks dividing up the mail and giving it to each carrier, the warehouse-like building they worked in with the giant skylights serving as the only indication of the weather outside. She remembered being petrified on her first day—just out of college with a history degree and uncertain of her prospects. The civil service exam had come up and on a lark she took it. Next thing she knew she was a mailman. Twelve years later, she was teaching another young woman how to put pieces of paper into little metal boxes. She smiled ruefully, wondering if she should tell Georgianna to either run for the hills or settle into a well-paid, pension-promised life of monotony.

Chapter Seven

By the following week, Chris had George, as Georgianna preferred to be called, on an auxiliary route that bordered her route. The mail volume was light and they decided to meet for lunch at the Zoo. Not only was George a quick learner, but she was also a member of the Dark Side, which was the term coined by postal workers for lesbians. The Fat Boy Club had already accused Chris of favoritism.

Her retort was standard. "How else do you expect us to take over the world? We advance our own kind."

They never knew whether to take her seriously or not, so they went back to eating their breakfast burritos.

At noon they sauntered into the Zoo to find Amadeus and Midge poring over a book. Amadeus was behind the bar and Midge sat on the customer side. "See, this isn't so bad," Midge said.

"At least it's humorous." Amadeus put the book down and looked inquisitively at Chris.

"Amadeus and Midge, meet George."

"Nice to meet you," Amadeus said, sticking out her hand. George shook it. Midge did the same.

Rose came out from the kitchen with two boxed-up sandwiches. "I didn't know if you two would have time to sit down and eat so I made them to go just in case."

"Actually, we're running ahead of schedule. Rose, this is George, our new hire."

"Hi," they said in unison. They didn't take their eyes off each other. Chris swore she saw sparks fly between them. They started talking shop. Apparently George had spent a lot of time as a waitress before she started with the post office.

"So what's this?" Chris asked, opening the book that Amadeus had set down.

"It's for the book club next week. Here's your copy," Amadeus said, pulling it out from behind the bar.

"We're starting already, how wonderful," Chris said. This was Date Night Club's first highbrow attempt at meeting quality people. A lesbian book group with monthly meetings and a reading list seemed like a good start.

Amadeus rolled her eyes at Chris's obvious attempt at putting positive spin on the situation. "I'm not a big reader."

Chris noticed the bookmark was set in about ten pages.

"Luce got us set up," Midge said. She closed her book and had a faraway look as if still engrossed in it.

Chris studied the cover. It was a book of lesbian fiction by Alex Taylor titled *The Heiress*. She read the jacket cover. "It sounds interesting."

"It's funny. I like funny lesbians," Midge said.

"They do seem to be a rare breed," Chris replied.

Midge was still wearing her checkered chef's pants but she had taken off her smock. Underneath she had a tie-dyed T-shirt of bright blue and green swirls.

"That's a great shirt," Chris said.

"Thank you. I'm just an old hippie at heart." Midge tucked an errant curl behind her ear.

Chris opened the Styrofoam container for George and shoved it in her direction. "You need to eat."

"I should get back to work," Rose said. She studiously avoided Amadeus's gaze.

"Call me," George said, quickly scribbling her name on a cocktail napkin.

"I will."

Amadeus let out a heavy sigh. "How come it's not that easy for us?"

Chris swiveled around on her barstool. "Is she here?"

"Who?" Amadeus asked, absently running a finger through one of her red curls.

"The love of your life."

"How the hell would I know? I'm not even sure I want to look for her."

"That's why it's not easy for us."

"We have expectations," Midge said.

Chris took a bite of her sandwich. Rose had doubled up on the provolone. She looked over at George, who was eating her lunch and watching Rose as she got drinks for the couple at the end of the bar.

"How's your lunch?" Chris asked.

"Fabulous," George replied.

"I'm sure."

Amadeus opened the book again and then quickly shut it. "I don't have the attention span for this."

Midge was already engrossed in her copy of the book.

"Go to the gym and get on a bike. It'll help. You can read and the spinning will keep your left brain busy. Besides, you can check out the classes at the health club as another potential dating spot," Chris suggested.

"I don't know about this pack mentality. I'm kind of a do-it-yourself gal," Amadeus said.

"And you've been doing it badly. As a lesbian, it's your duty to be pack-oriented. Look around you. Lesbians travel in groups of two, four, six or more. Can't you make concessions?" Chris said.

"Now you employ another tactic—guilt," Amadeus said. She picked up the book. "I'm going to the gym."

"Thank you," Chris said.

"I'm only doing this for B."

Later that evening, Chris sat in her La-Z-Boy chair with a pile of papers on her lap. She tapped them with her pen. She was stuck. She had no idea how she was going to save the naked postal worker his job. As the union steward it was her responsibility to do her best to represent him. Still, spanking it on the job was not normal behavior and she found the whole thing embarrassing.

The front door slammed and B. came bustling in. "Sorry, I can't get used to that door. I think it needs a new spring." She was carrying two grocery bags stuffed full of food.

"What's up?" Chris said, getting up to help her. She grabbed one of the bags.

"I'm going to make you dinner. I bet it's been a while since you've had a home-cooked meal."

"It has." Chris carried the bag to the kitchen. Her kitchen was small but well organized. She'd updated all the appliances and put in granite countertops. She didn't use it a lot but it looked good.

"What were you working on?" B. grabbed the sour cream, the pork roast and butter and put them in the fridge. She straightened out the fridge while she was at it—like the butter wouldn't be happy if it was sitting next to the pickles. Everything was lined up, right down to the tomatoes that were set up like pool balls in the crisper. It was starting to creep Chris out.

B. had also lined up the pantry. All the labels faced forward. The canned items were arranged according to type of food—peas, corn, beans were grouped together. Canned soup functioned as one unit, pasta another, while juices, bottled water and Gatorade were displayed in the same fashion. Chris had mentioned this behavior to Luce, who explained that it was a coping mechanism. She advised Chris not to mention it to B.

"Is it something for work?" B. asked.

"Yeah, this guy got caught spanking it and then stood naked except for his socks on a customer's porch. He got fired and it's my job to get him rehired."

"That's going to be a tough one." B. put the cornmeal and pinto beans on the counter.

Chris got them both a Corona and chopped up a lime. She shoved a slice in each bottle and handed one to B.

"Thank you," B. said. She clinked her bottle with Chris's. "And thanks for letting me stay here."

"I enjoy your company, B. It gets kind of old living alone."

"You mean you look forward to me coming home?"

"I do."

"Your uniform, it's completely regulation, right?"

"It's supposed to be." Chris couldn't figure out where B. was going. She got out a big pot for the beans. They would need to cook for a while.

"Right down to the shoes and socks?"

"Yes."

"Was he wearing regulation socks?"

"I don't think so. Regulation socks are about eight bucks a pair. It's a waste of your uniform allowance. Most of us buy cheap gym socks." Chris picked up the cilantro. "Do you want me to chop this up?"

"Please. Rinse it good. I got it at the farmer's market."

Chris pulled out a strainer, dumped the cilantro in it and gave it a good soaking. B. was right—it still had a lot of field dirt attached to it.

B. put the pinto beans in a large pot and filled it with water. "So I was thinking if he wasn't in uniform and he was on his lunch hour, that technically isn't on the clock. It's non-postal time, right?"

Chris was getting the gist of where B. was going. "That's correct."

"Is there something in your rules and regulations—what's it called?"

"The M forty-one."

"That states only certain activities can be done at lunchtime?" B. spiced the beans with garlic and salt, dumped some of the cilantro in and put a lid on the pot.

"No, there's not. It's a thirty-minute period when management assumes we're eating lunch."

"I think you could make this his lunch hour, which removes him from postal regulations. The indecent exposure charge will stick but if one wants to commit a misdemeanor on his or her lunch hour that should be no one's business."

"We've had people caught with drugs, charged with a felony, and still got their jobs back after doing time."

"Exactly. What's a little crazy nudity in comparison?"

"If they fire him for that when others have done worse, we can get them for disparity of treatment and file an EEOC." Chris gave a B. a big hug. "You're brilliant."

"And I'm a great cook," B. said.

"Yes, you are."

"I talked to Jordan this morning," B. said as she chopped up onions. She didn't look at Chris.

"B., you shouldn't have. Diane warned you to stay away from her."

"I know, but I miss her so much. I had a courier deliver her a cell phone when Diane went out shopping. It's our secret." B. started mixing the tortilla dough. She looked down at her camel-colored Ultrasuede business suit as the first flecks of flour landed on it. She briskly washed her hands and removed her blazer. Chris found her an apron.

"You better hope Diane doesn't find out," Chris said.

"She won't. Jordan is sneaky just like me. She's on my side."

"Jordan is a six-year-old child whose opinions change on the hour."

"I'm not letting her go without a fight. That kid has been the best thing that ever happened to me." B. started to sniffle.

Chris held her. She refrained from suggesting B. should have treated the kid's mother better. She knew B. had never been mean to Diane. Her sin, Chris decided, was her personality—an obsessive-compulsive overachiever who was inattentive to anyone else's needs. Having discovered this tidbit of psychobabble from her unconscious, Chris was loathe to do anything about it. Perhaps she could talk to Luce and figure out a way to perform some miraculous behavior modification. "It'll be all right," she said.

B. straightened up. She pulled a pocket pack of Kleenex from her trousers and blew her nose. "Of course it will. I'm a survivor and I have a spy."

Chris smiled. She did her best not to look worried.

B. went back to mixing the tortilla dough. Chris dug around and found her tortilla press. The kitchen was soon filled with the smell of native cuisine. Chris was reminded of other days when she too had been part of a couple. Cooking for one was depressing. That was how she came to eat at the Zoo so often. "This smells fabulous."

"Wait until you taste it."

The next day Chris sat in the manager's office with the head of personnel and the union president, Richard Griego.

"I'm supposed to let him come back to work because he was

at lunch when the aforementioned act was performed," said Ray Romero, the head of personnel. He was a snippy little man with black, slicked-back hair and tidy brown suit.

"Basically," Chris said. She looked over at Richard. He was a Hispanic man in his mid-forties, his dark hair graying at the temples. He stroked his neatly trimmed goatee. It was a well-documented mannerism indicating he was about to bring out the big guns.

Richard said, "Ray, I don't need to remind you that we have had over the years several dozen employees who've had run-ins with the law and still retained their positions. To single this one out is just asking for an expensive EEOC. He'll get administrative leave and a settlement when we win the case. I don't think you want that."

Ray pulled out a calculator from his black leather briefcase and a postal form along with a yellow notepad. He did some scribbling and number crunching.

Chris looked over at Richard who winked and nodded. It was going to be all right.

"This is the deal. We give him a two-week suspension without pay and he takes a mandatory reassignment. He's blacklisted from this station, understood," Ray said, staring at both of them with his beady little eyes. He looked like a prairie dog with a bad disposition.

"I find that acceptable," Richard said. "Chris?"

"It works for me."

Ray handed them each a postal form to sign off on. Then he got up and clicked his briefcase shut. "I'd advise you to inform your union members to keep their hands off their private parts during lunch."

Richard laughed heartily. "Sure thing, Romero."

"What a dick," Chris muttered under her breath after Ray left.

"It doesn't matter. We got Taylor his job back. That's all that counts. Good legwork."

"I had help."

Sid, the supervisor, came up to them. "Did you get him off?"

"We're not allowed to do that anymore, remember," Chris said.

They all laughed.

"Until next time," Richard said, tugging on his earlobe in his signature Carol Burnett move.

Chris smiled and shook his hand. "Thanks again."

"My pleasure. See you, Sid."

Chris couldn't wait to tell B. that her plan worked. B. was still depressed and a success like this would help.

Chapter Eight

"Oh, this is going to be fun," B. said.

"I can hardly wait," Amadeus let out an overdramatic squeal of delight.

Chris gave her the you-better-behave-yourself look. Amadeus pointedly ignored her.

They had all congregated at the Zoo and would carpool to the book club meeting. They'd been advised by the bookstore that parking was an issue. The reading club would be held once a month each second Thursday. This seemed manageable, Chris thought. She could read one book a month. She was worried about Amadeus's commitment but if she had to write Cliff's Notes for Amadeus she would.

"I've taken the liberty of drawing up a basic outline of the story in order to help with the discussion. We don't want to look like the dummy group. I've heard these book groupies can be like sharks at the tuna fest." B. handed them each a copy.

Chris hoped B.'s idea of a metaphor improved over the tuna fest. They shouldn't even use the word *tuna* in the presence of lesbians—it was downright dangerous. She had read the book and found it amusing, but she wasn't one for dissecting it. The story was what it said. Who was she to pick apart the writer's intentions? Couldn't the story be just that?

Luce leaned over and whispered, "It's good for her to have another focus."

"I know."

"This is great, B. Thanks for all the hard work," Luce said.

"Yes, very thoughtful," Midge piped in. She pulled a mechanical pencil from the breast pocket of her tweed jacket and jotted a few notes of her own in the margins of B.'s outline.

Chris watched her, wondering if sitting next to Midge might be a good idea. She noticed Midge's outfit. She looked like a miniature version of an English country squire, with her tweed jacket complete with leather elbow patches, tan slacks, a white silk shirt and burgundy cravat. "You're looking quite dapper this evening."

"I'm dressed for the part. People stare at me anyway so I might as well give them something good to look at," Midge said.

Chris laughed. "I love you, Midge."

"You are an inspiration," Luce said.

Chris caught Amadeus studying her own fashion choice. "We can buzz by the loft and you can change." Amadeus lived downtown in a swanky loft apartment.

"What's wrong with my outfit?"

"Nothing," Chris replied.

"There must be something or you wouldn't have said anything."

"A blue polo and khaki trousers with topsiders just shouts utilitarian, that's all."

"What are you implying? I'm boring?" She had raised her voice and several patrons seated near the bar stared.

"Amadeus, you look stunning," Luce said, giving Chris a pointed look.

"What are you—wanna-be hippie girl?" Amadeus said in a lower tone of voice. She was referring to Chris's tie-dyed T-shirt and Levi's cutoffs.

"Midge gave me this shirt." Chris knew she'd won the match. She'd cornered Amadeus.

"It's a nice shirt."

"Let it go. Chris is picking on you because she's nervous. This is her way of handling it," B. said. Chris started to protest but B. put her hand up.

Chris stopped to think. "She's right. I'm just fucking with you because I'm not good at stuff like this."

"Me either," Amadeus said.

"I'll sit between you two and serve as your mentor. The group won't notice if I do all the talking. Now, we'd best get going," Midge said, checking her watch.

They piled into B.'s Lexus. It was a tight fit but it beat trying to find spots for five cars. B. headed down Juan Tabo toward Menaul and the bookstore. Everyone was quiet as they listened to B.'s musical choice of sad love songs. B. didn't cry, but Chris could tell she was getting blue.

Amadeus, who was sitting up front with her, looked over at B. and said, "Why are you listening to this crap when it makes you miserable?"

"It's like therapy."

"No, it's nothing more than self-pity and masochism." Amadeus rolled down her window, ejected the CD and threw it out.

Chris started to laugh. She looked over at Luce and Midge, who were both mortified, and then they too started to laugh.

B. almost rear-ended the car in front of her. "I don't think that was necessary."

"It was. Trust me," Amadeus said. "I'll buy you a happy CD of your choice."

B. nodded. "Maybe it is time leave off the weepy stuff."

"I don't think I can do this," Amadeus said.

"What's wrong now?" Chris said.

"I'm having a flashback to English lit class where people say 'it struck me' and use vocabulary words that don't fit easily into everyday discourse."

Chris laughed. "Discourse?"

"Crap, they weren't kidding about the parking," B. said as they approached the bookstore.

"You'll be fine, Amadeus. Besides, your dream girl might be sitting in the chair next to you. People like listeners. The world has way too many talkers in it."

"That's right. Be the strong and silent type," Midge said.

"That I can do."

"We'll just have to walk." B. had finally located a parking spot half a block from the bookstore.

They got out of the Lexus and headed toward the bookstore.

"I hear the author will be present tonight," Midge said, taking a beautiful silver and black Mont Blanc pen from her breast pocket. She clipped it to the front of the book.

"An autograph?" Chris said.

"I have great admiration for the creative mind," Midge replied.

The night had grown cool and Chris hoped the bookstore wasn't big on air conditioning. She hated being in places that insisted on keeping the temperature like a meat locker. She should have brought a sweatshirt.

"Maybe that explains the parking situation," B. glanced back at her car with consternation.

"The car will be fine," Luce said. She wrapped her arm in B.'s and gave it a comforting pat.

"You're right," B. said, straightening her shoulders. "It is only a car, after all."

Amadeus got close to Chris and whispered, "I didn't get to finish the book. How did it end?"

"She gets the girl but Anne gets outed. She lives up to the challenge, though," Chris replied.

"I knew she would. I think I identify with her character the most," Amadeus said.

"Remember to preface that statement with 'it strikes me.'"

"Oh, yes, that's right."

"I was only kidding about your outfit. You look lovely as usual."

Amadeus smiled. "Thank you. I don't think I'll find anyone here. Book people aren't really my type."

"I know, but someone else might," Chris said, looking at the rest of the group.

"Like a short bookworm?"

"Exactly." Chris smirked, thinking they must be quite a sight: a red-headed Amazon, a Dolly Parton businesswoman, a hippie artist and a midget. She couldn't find any adjectives for herself other than a woman who'd made bad choices. *Well, we definitely cover the spectrum of lesbianism.* Tonight had potential.

The book group was set up in the back. Chairs were organized in a circle and most of them were already full, even though it was only quarter of seven. The crowd was as diverse as they were. A couple of women moved over so the five of them could sit together. Amadeus sat on the end. A petite dark-haired woman sat next to her. Amadeus nodded her greeting.

Chris nudged her. In a low voice she said, "We're supposed to be meeting people. Nodding doesn't count."

Amadeus gave her a dirty look, which would have potentially been followed by a nasty retort except that she was interrupted by the book group leader. "We'll start in about ten minutes."

She was a tall woman with mousy brown hair pulled back in a ponytail. She wore fashionable dark-rimmed glasses, a tweed vest and Birkenstock sandals. She appeared to take her job very seriously. *Pity she's not short*, Chris thought. She'd be a good match for Midge. They both were wearing tweed in the middle of May in the high desert—that had to count for something.

It suddenly occurred to Chris that she was in over her head, beyond her ken, out of her league. What did she know about orchestrating love lives? Her own was a complete disaster. Her bolder self took hold. So she didn't know shit. When had that ever stopped her? She looked around the room.

There was a handsome Hispanic butch dressed in black Levi's and a royal-blue dress shirt. She was checking out B. Chris nudged B. She smiled back at the woman. Chris got up and introduced herself and then said, "This is my friend Bernadette."

"Jude. Nice to meet you." Her eyes never left B.'s face.

"Why don't we switch places?" Chris suggested.

"Sure." Jude moved over.

Chris found herself seated next to two blond spiky-haired women. They looked like a couple—similar hair, similar dress and the same speech patterns. This always creeped her out. Did it have to be like this?

"These are my friends Holly and Ariana," Jude said.

"It's a pleasure to meet you," Chris replied.

"Charmed," B. said, giving them a good once-over.

Chris could tell she was sizing them up.

"They're trying to get me out more—to meet people," Jude told B.

"That's exactly what we're up to," B. replied. She leaned toward Jude, who was trying hard not to fasten her gaze on B.'s prominent cleavage. Chris chuckled to herself as the boobs won the battle. B. whispered, "Are they together?"

"Only for a hundred years."

Holly smiled at Jude sweetly. "Yes, we've been domestic forever."

"That's admirable," Chris piped in.

"How about you?" Ariana asked, her piercing blue eyes boring a hole in Chris's psyche like a laser.

"I'm single. I've just never found the right one, I guess."

"She prefers nymphomaniacs to real people," Amadeus said.

Chris gave her a dirty look.

"It beats the lockbox type," added the petite brunette who was sitting on the other side of Amadeus.

Chris beamed at her. "Thank you."

All further conversation came to a halt as the book group leader took the floor.

"Hello, everyone, my name is Ulma and I'm your book group coordinator. I want to thank everyone for coming tonight. It's so nice to know people, our people"—she clasped her hands together—"are still reading. These books are, after all, our legacy. They tell our stories and it's very important that we support our writers, the people who labor so ardently to bring our lives to the page."

The speech droned on, exceeding Chris's attention span. She noticed that Luce and Midge had moved, taking their chairs across the way. It might have had something to do with Jude's friends, the blond-haired couple. They had upset the seating arrangement by introducing their enormous deluxe camping chairs complete with cup holders. Chris fidgeted in hers. The room, instead of being the meat locker as she had expected, was warm and her thighs were sticking to the metal chair. Whoever invented the fold-up metal chair was a sadist, a near relative of Satan intent on torturing people trying to make themselves better by attending reading, lectures and the like.

The comfy-chair girls were regulars, as Ulma informed everyone. Everyone introduced herself. The petite brunette next to Amadeus introduced herself as Alex Taylor.

"As in the writer?" Chris inquired.

Alex nodded.

"Isn't this grand? She wanted to sit in and get some feedback from live readers," Ulma said, clasping her hands together again.

Chris muttered, "As in contrast to dead readers," and Alex smiled and tried not laugh.

"You don't look substantial enough to be a writer," Amadeus said.

"I didn't realize there was a size requirement," Alex replied.

Amadeus broke out laughing and slapped Alex on the back. Chris, being well aware of Amadeus's strength, put her outstretched arm in front of her to prevent the diminutive writer from sailing off her chair. As an amazon, Amadeus was potentially hazardous to small people. Chris was amazed that she hadn't killed or at least maimed Midge yet.

When Alex caught her breath she thanked Chris.

"So I have a question about the book," Ariana, one of the spiky blondes, said.

"Sure," Alex replied, straightening up her slightly askew T-shirt.

"I've read all your books and pickles appear in several of them."

"I've never noticed that."

Chris peered over at the blond couple. She got a bad vibe. Jude seemed all right, but those two clearly had an agenda. She could feel it. Jude and B. were smiling at each other. They seemed privy to something the rest of the group didn't know.

"Well, they do," said Holly, the second part of the couple from hell.

"Ladies, I don't really see where this is going," Ulma said.

"Pickles can be seen as a symbol. We all know how writers use certain themes and symbols in their work," Ariana replied.

B. snickered. Chris didn't get it. She looked at Luce and Midge for a clue.

"Perhaps she just likes pickles," Midge said matter-of-factly.

"I do like pickles, along with other foodstuffs that I'm sure figure prominently in my books," Alex replied.

"Pickles do have a long history in the culinary arts," Amadeus added.

Chris looked at the back of the book cover where a jar of pickles was displayed. Maybe there was something to this pickle thing.

"That's not what I'm talking about," Ariana said.

"Pickles are a phallic symbol and we want to know why a lesbian author has repeatedly used them in her novels, especially this last one, where the protagonist is a pickle heiress. I think I have a valid point here and I want it addressed," Holly said.

"You've outed yourself on this one, lady," Ariana said in a high-pitched voice.

"Excuse me?" Alex replied.

"Ariana and Holly, I think that's enough talk about a vegetable. I mean, it's really more like a condiment anyway," Ulma said.

"No, it's not. It's a Freudian slip. I think she's got a thing for male genitalia and she's trying to pollute the reader's mind with phallic symbols. This is a plot," Ariana said, her voice rising.

"To do what? Destroy the Lesbian Nation?" Chris said.

"Your hypothesis only pertains if there are references to strap-ons in her novels. Are there?" Luce asked.

"Well?" Ulma said, staring hard at them.

"Pickles are as good as," Holly retorted.

"The pickle heiress was meant to be funny," Alex said.

Chris could tell she was getting flustered. She was glad they had come as a group, just in case they had to save this poor woman from a lynching.

A woman from the outer circle piped up. "This is a romantic comedy, not a feminist thesis. She writes funny stuff, that's all."

"The pickles are always featured in the icebox. What does that tell you?" Ariana said.

"Any vacuum-sealed food item, once opened, needs to be refrigerated," Amadeus said.

Her disbelief evident, Alex looked over at Chris. "It's just a bad dream. It'll be over soon." She touched Alex's arm.

"Why do you two always do this to me?" Ulma said, her upper lip quivering.

"Do what?" Holly said, glaring at Ulma.

"Turn everything into an argument that has phallic overtones," Ulma replied.

"Yeah, you two are always the ones bringing up the dick angle," someone from the back called out.

"Gross!" said another book group member.

"Maybe you two are the ones with the problem," someone else said.

"What's that supposed to mean?" Holly said, getting out of her chair.

"Like you wish you had one."

"She probably has a whole drawerful," another woman taunted.

"I do not," Holly said.

"Ladies, that's enough. We don't need to go there," Ulma said.

Alex let out a heavy sigh and rubbed her temples. "This wasn't what I had in mind."

"You wanted feedback," Chris said, shrugging her shoulders.

"Not like this."

"Let's go get a drink. My friend owns the Zoo and they've got fabulous martinis."

"I think that's a good idea. Your friends aren't part of that?" She pointed to the group in the middle of the room, where a shouting match had broken out while Ulma tried to regain control.

"No, they're sitting quietly."

It was true. They were watching the whole episode in amazement, and to think Amadeus thought this was going to be boring. This was better than mud wrestling and more politically correct, Chris thought. She gave them hand signals. They nodded. Chris caught Jude by the arm. "Why don't you come with us?"

"If it's all right," Jude said, looking over at B.

B. smiled back. "It would mean the book club wasn't a total wash."

Jude beamed. "Then I'd love to."

No one appeared to notice them as they slinked out. Ariana was yelling something about the world being covered in penis juice because most men don't wash their hands after going to the restroom. That was enough talk about boy parts, Chris decided. Who would have thought something as harmless as a book group could go so wrong?

"Pickles causing such an uproar," Chris said, shaking her head.

Alex smiled. "I'll make certain they appear scattered throughout all my work. I have a new symbol."

"Symbol and theme are underused these days. I commend your efforts," Midge said.

Alex raised her eyebrows.

"Alex, meet Midge. She'll give you some credible feedback," Chris said.

Chapter Nine

"Pippy, it's all right, girl," Chris said as she pulled the sales ad from her satchel. The Pipster—her pet name for the dog—was a small German shepherd. She was going berserk and pulling on the leg of the lawn chair of Mr. Gutierrez. He was always waiting for his sales ad that Chris delivered every Tuesday afternoon. As a bargain hunter, he made all his purchases according to what was on sale that week.

"Hi, Mr. G.," Chris said as she approached him. There was no response. Chris leaned down to scratch the dog's ears. Mr. G. was sitting perfectly straight with his eyes wide open. "Mr. G., are you . . ." She touched his arm. He was stone cold. "Oh, no." She put her fingers on his neck. There was no pulse. "Oh, shit!" She sat down next to the dog and untied her. "It's going to be fine, girl."

She pulled out her cell phone and called 911. Then she called the station and told them she was going to be late. Sid was sympathetic. The mailman was often the first person to find an elderly person living alone dead. It was an occupational hazard.

The police car pulled up and a female officer got out. The dog went wild. Chris grabbed her leash and pulled her back.

"That his dog?" she asked, pulling out her pad.

"Yes."

"You just find him?" the red-headed officer continued.

"Yeah. He's kind of stiff."

"Rigor already set in."

The ambulance came down the street but didn't have the siren going. There wouldn't be a hurry to get this one help, Chris thought.

Chris gave the officer her statement as they loaded Mr. Gutierrez into the ambulance. "What will happen to the dog?" Chris asked as she stroked the Pipster's ears.

"Animal Control will take her to the shelter," the police officer said.

"Could I take her? I don't think he has any family and the dog has some behavior issues. She wouldn't make a good family dog," Chris said.

"You don't want her put down."

"No, I'd rather give her a home. I don't have any other animals or kids, so her issues wouldn't be a problem," Chris said. She did have a picky roommate at the moment, but B. would just have to get over it.

"I don't see why not," the officer said. "It's less paperwork."

"Great, thanks a lot." She pulled on the Pipster's leash. "Come on, girl. You're coming with me."

The Pipster stopped in her tracks and let out a terrific howl like a death wail and then went willingly with Chris. She put the dog in the cargo area of the postal vehicle and quickly finished her route. The dog lay down in the back and went to sleep. It must have been a hard day for her.

When she got back to the station she tied the dog to the handlebars of her motorcycle. She got her some water and bought a Slim Jim from the vending machine. Pipster drank and ate hurriedly, as if she wasn't certain where her next meal was coming from. Chris knelt down by her. "Don't worry, baby. I'll take care of you." She went inside again, turned in her keys and accountable mail and clocked out. She hadn't quite figured out how she was going to get the dog home on her motorcycle. She thought her satchel was her best bet.

The Pipster was ecstatic at her return. She was obviously traumatized at losing her master. Chris slipped the satchel over her shoulder and then wheeled her motorcycle next to the concrete picnic table. She swung the satchel around so that it sat firmly on the passenger part of her motorcycle seat. She called the dog, enticing her with a piece of Slim Jim. The dog jumped up on the bench.

"C'mon, get in," Chris said, pointing at the satchel. She patted the bag. "It's safe, I hope." She started the bike as an added incentive. The Pipster barked. "Look, we don't have a lot of room for negotiation here." She started to pull away. The dog jumped in the bag. Chris reached around and gave her a pat on the head. "This might work. Don't worry. I'll go slow."

She took off slowly. The dog leaned into her back and licked her ear.

"You're welcome, sweetie."

They made it home safely and without incident, aside from the amazed stares of the people they passed. The Pipster hopped out of the satchel and took a big poop in Chris's front yard.

"Why do I get the feeling you're going to dramatically change my life?" Chris said as she watched the dog scratch the rocks in Chris's perfectly landscaped front yard, sending gravel flying to mark her territory. The Pipster barked at her again. "Oh, and you're going to be sassy too."

Chris let them both in the house. The Pipster immediately

jumped on the couch, put her face between her paws and let out a heavy sigh.

"Don't get too comfortable. We have to go shopping."

She dug out her cell phone and called B.

"What's up?" B. asked. She had picked up on the first ring. The woman was amazing, Chris thought.

"When can you come home?"

"Why? Do you need me?"

"Yes. We have to go shopping for our new roommate."

"We have a new roommate. Do I have to move out?" Is she your new lover? Is she cute?"

"No, you don't have to move. She's just a friend in need and yes, she's cute."

"Great. I'll be right there."

Fifteen minutes later, B. was standing in the living room, staring at the dog. "This is our new roommate?"

"Isn't she cute? She needs some provisions. I was thinking PetSmart."

The Pipster came over and nudged B.'s hand, her brown almond-shaped eyes gazing up at her. She knew how to play needy. Chris was impressed.

B. knelt down to pet her. "You are cute."

The Pipster rolled on her back so B. could pet her stomach.

"Oh, how sweet."

"I'm glad you like her, because it's here or the shelter. She's not usually this friendly."

"She's just misunderstood. What's her name?"

"The Pipster." Chris grabbed a pencil and paper. She wanted to make a list.

"The Pipster? Why the added article?"

"Wait and see. She's got quite an attitude for a midget dog."

"She's not a midget."

"B., she weighs all of thirty pounds. Don't you think that's a little small for a German shepherd?"

B. stood up and took a good look at her. "I guess you are kind of small."

They loaded the dog into B.'s Lexus. She sat straight up in the backseat and was very quiet. She watched the cars go by as they headed up Central and she kept eyeing Chris.

It dawned on her that the Pipster thought they were taking her to the pound. Mr. G. had rescued her from the pound so she'd been dumped off once already in her life. "Don't worry, Pippy, we're going someplace nice. You're ours now. No more pound." Chris rubbed her head, trying to reassure her. The dog crawled up between them, putting her head on the console. Chris scratched her ears. "You'll like this place."

B. turned onto Eubank. "Now, where is it?"

"Almost to the freeway in that strip mall."

"By Wal-Mart?" B.'s eyes got big.

"Parking in front of PetSmart isn't like the Wal-Mart parking lot, I swear." Chris tried to keep a knowing smile from creeping across her face. B. had almost been flattened by a group of overeager seniors once. She compared it to the running of the bulls in Spain.

"Right here is good." She pointed to a spot close to edge of the lot and watched as B. peeled her fingers off the steering wheel. *Great*, she thought, *I've got a Wal-Mart freak and a goofy dog.*

They got out of the car. Chris hooked up the Pipster's leash. She could tell the dog was trying to figure out where they were going. Deciding it wasn't the shelter, the Pipster moved forward with the attitude of a Dale Carnegie graduate. *Well, this is a good sign*, Chris thought. B. was still eyeing the adjacent Wal-Mart parking lot.

Chris attempted to distract her. "Have you heard from Jude?"

B. smiled. "Of course. We went to lunch at the Melting Pot. Did you know she's a civil engineer?"

"Uh, no, I didn't."

"I told her I was healing."

"Upfront is good," Chris replied as they made their way to the front door of PetSmart.

"I felt it the only correct thing to do. She said she admired my integrity."

"But she wondered if you two could be friends," Chris said.

Clearly stunned, B. looked at her. "Yes, she did."

"That's great," Chris replied. She didn't want to elaborate. B. was naïve when it came to women. Chris was always forced to play mama coyote to the lesbian pack. She would wait. She would study Jude's behavior and pounce if necessary.

"All right then, Pippy, let's go," she said, leading the dog and B. into PetSmart. The dog lagged behind, still uncertain. Chris gave the leash a tug. A Rhodesian ridgeback and his owner passed by. The Pipster snarled and growled. The other dog stuck his tail between his legs and slinked past.

B. was delighted. "I like her style. You go, girl. Head up, shoulders back, tell the world you are here."

Chris let out a heavy sigh.

B. grabbed a cart and the dog jumped at the side of it. "Oh, you want in?" B. lifted her up into the cart. The Pipster put her front legs on the edge of the cart and barked like she was the captain of the ship. "Isn't she cute?" B. doted.

The clerk, a vivacious brunette, smiled at them as they strolled by. She was dressed in black pants and a green polo shirt, the uniform for store employees; she filled hers out better than most, however, with her perky round breasts and flat stomach.

B. must had been watching because she leaned into Chris and said, "Maybe this dog thing will work in your favor."

"Meaning?"

"She's very attractive."

"I don't know what you're talking about," Chris replied, making a show of studying the aisle marquees.

"Right," B. said.

In their apparent disregard of their charge, the Pipster had snagged a package of tennis balls off one of the square sale tables and was ripping open the plastic bag.

"What the hell?" Chris said, pulling at the package of balls. A tug-of-war ensued.

The sexy clerk came over to help. "It appears she's a ball girl." Her gaze met Chris's. She picked up one of the yellow tennis balls that had fallen into the cart and handed it to the Pipster, who instantly dropped the package in order to snag the lone ball. "She would benefit from some obedience training."

Chris nodded.

"We have a preliminary class to see if the dogs qualify. It only takes twenty minutes. You might want to give it a try."

"Qualify?" Chris said.

"Of course she'll qualify. She's a highly intelligent dog," B. said.

"Great, I teach the class and I'd love to have you in it." The woman extended her hand. "I'm Kate, by the way."

"I'm Chris and this is my friend B. and this is the Pipster."

"The Pipster," Kate raised her eyebrow. "We might have to lose the definite article."

B. stiffened. "Perhaps you should reserve judgment on that. C'mon, Chris, we've got some shopping to do before class."

"Sure," Chris replied, slightly bewildered by the macho-estrogen battle she'd witnessed. It was a pissing contest, as the boys at work called it.

B. wheeled the cart down the dog food aisle, picked the most expensive brand of dry food and the same in wet food. Then she took them to the treats aisle and let the Pipster sniff boxes until they came upon just the right kind. A new leash of royal blue, a matching collar, several more bags of tennis balls, a cedar-chip bed and pillow with bones on it, and B. was satisfied. They stood in line at the checkout counter. B. handed the clerk her credit card, giving Chris the do-not-protest look. Chris shrugged.

Then she instructed Chris to take the purchases to the car while she made the Pipster an identification tag. "We don't want her getting lost. We still have five minutes until showtime." She tossed Chris the keys to the car. Chris hurried out.

Chris loaded the stuff in B.'s trunk and walked back toward the store. She had a feeling that no matter how attractive Kate was, this class thing was going to turn out badly. It was times like these that she missed Luce. Luce was sane but she was also out of town at the moment. She was doing some art festivals in Arizona and wouldn't be back for a week. So she was going to have to wing it on her own. At least it would be a good story. She and Luce could sip wine and watch the sun set over the Sandias while Chris regaled her with the tale of the Pipster's first shopping trip and class.

Chris was still in la-la land as she approached the training arena. B. had lifted the Pipster from the cart and was attempting introductions with the other dogs in the class. There was much tail-wagging and butt-sniffing except for the Pipster. She was standing in the middle of the arena with a ball in her mouth and emitting a low growl.

Kate, the instructor, took offense at this. "She's not allowed to do that."

B. clenched the leash in her hand. "And why not? She's simply asserting her superiority."

Kate straightened her shoulders and cocked her neck to one side. It cracked like a pepper grinder.

This isn't good, Chris thought as she stood at the edge of the group.

"Bring her here. She needs to know this is a friendly learning environment, not a dominance session."

B. didn't budge. "Maybe she doesn't feel that way."

Kate grabbed the leash. "She doesn't get to have an opinion. Chris, I want you to be her partner, her leader." She handed the leash to Chris, who obediently took it. She was busy casting an apologetic look at B., who was still glowering at Kate, when the disturbance began.

Kate was giving her training speech when the Pipster sidled up next to her. Then the dog jerked the leash out of Chris's hand and made two quick passes around Kate's calves, essentially hog-tying her before anyone knew what had happened. The dog took one last look at the dominatrix, and while Chris yelled, "No, please don't do it," she took off.

Kate hit the floor with a thud and the Pipster's collar snapped off. She made a run for it.

"B., go get her," Chris said. She untangled the leash and tried to help Kate up. She was fuming. "I'm so sorry."

"That dog is evil." Kate was seething.

Chris made her own run for it. Once outside, she looked around frantically for B. and the Pipster. She heard a horn. B. was in the car. Chris made for the car and hopped in. "Did you find her?"

B. pulled out of the parking spot. She cocked her head toward the backseat. The Pipster was on the floor in the back looking like the perfect fugitive, although she was gently biting on her tennis ball like it was a pacifier. "She was waiting by the car."

"Holy crap, B., she's only been in our lives for an afternoon and already she's up for assault and battery."

B. turned out on to Eubank, checking the rearview mirror to see if they were being followed. "Yes, well, but we didn't register for the class and I'm sure worse things have happened."

"Like what? Mass murder?" Chris said.

The Pipster must have sensed it was all right to get up. She poked her head in between the front seats and licked them both on the cheek.

"See, she's apologizing. I like you. You've got spunk. Now, where's that dog park?" B. clicked on the button for her OnStar and got directions from the operator.

"Aren't we rewarding bad behavior?" Chris asked.

"Nonsense. We just have to find the thing that inspires her. Obviously, learning stupid tricks isn't her gig."

"Inspires her?" Chris was beginning to feel like she was way out of her league. She wasn't parental material and suddenly, with B.'s help, the Pipster had become a furry child.

"Everyone has a thing that makes them rise up to the challenge, which in turn allows them to excel and reach their full potential."

"B., this is a dog."

"So?" B. turned into the dog park. The Pipster was panting and racing back and forth in the backseat. B. raised her eyebrows in vindication.

"Let's be careful. We don't need any further infractions," Chris said.

"Of course. Come on, Pippy," B. said, opening the door. The Pipster hopped out with the tennis ball in her mouth.

The dog park looked like any other park except that there were dogs instead of kids running around. Chris swore the Pipster looked up at them with a smile, her eyes shining with gratitude.

"See, this is more her style," B. said. She opened the gate and let the dog through. She took off her leash and said, "Be free."

B. marched with the dog into the middle of the park. Chris trailed along, looking out for any potential hazards. The Pipster stopped, dropped the tennis ball and nudged it toward Chris, who figured she must have looked more like a softball player than B. Chris picked it up. The dog's eyes never left the ball. "Are you ready?"

The Pipster barked. Chris threw it as hard as she could. The dog took off. The little dog could fly, Chris thought. The ball bounced once and the Pipster leapt up in the air and caught it.

"I'd say she was a ball girl," B. said.

The Pipster ran back and dropped the ball at Chris's feet. She threw it again and again. Each time it seemed the dog got better at leaping and catching. B. made a few calls but was more attentive to the present moment than Chris had seen her in years. Maybe the Pipster was a good thing after all.

As they made their way back to the car, they passed a group of people and dogs playing on a training course. It looked like a relay race involving dogs and balls.

B. poked Chris. "The Pipster can run faster than those dogs." "You think so?"

"Watch. Wait until the next dog gets ready to run, then throw the ball for Pippy."

Chris lined them up so she and the Pipster were parallel to the course. She threw at the same time as the other dog ran. The Pipster took off. She beat the other dog by half a length.

"What'd I tell you," B. said. She removed her camel-colored blazer. The afternoon had grown warm.

"Let's try it again. It could have been a bench-warmer dog." B. scoffed.

Chris resumed her experiment. B. was right. Pippy was amazingly fast. The coach of the team noticed as well. She came over to Chris.

"You're dog is really good with a ball," the woman said.

Chris turned to find a long-legged blue-eyed blonde wearing a black Nike get-up. She had a matching ball cap and ponytail down her back. "She does seem to like it," Chris said, trying to be nonchalant. The blonde was stunning.

"So how does the game work?" B. interjected. She didn't seem as impressed with the woman's looks.

"It's called fly ball, like in baseball. Each team runs its dog in a timed race. The fastest total time wins."

"What about those jump things?" B. said.

"The height is determined by the shortest dog on the team."

This information appeared to be clicking in B.'s head as Chris and the coach pretended not to be checking each other out. Chris wished she had the gumption to say, "Look, I think you're really hot and I'd like to spend some mattress time with you." Then she felt like slapping herself, realizing she was slipping back into her old bad habit of cruising women just to get laid.

"So let me get this straight. A short, fast dog is best," B. said.

"Exactly. My name is Lola."

"I'm Chris and this is my friend B."

"Maybe your dog could give it a try. What's her name?"

"The Pipster. I don't know if that's a good idea," Chris said, suddenly hesitant.

"What are the requirements?" B. asked.

"The dog has to have some working knowledge of the basic obedience commands."

There's that word again, Chris thought. *Obedience.*

"Which are?" B. asked.

Chris noticed the way B. was eyeing the Pipster as she worked on her footwork with the tennis ball. She'd seen that look too many times before and it didn't bode well. It was her don't-tell-me-I-can't-do-something look.

"Sit, stay, lie down and come," Lola said.

"She can do that."

"B., can I talk to you for a minute?" Chris said to Lola, "We'll be right back." When they were out of earshot, Chris said, "B., may I remind you that we just got thrown out of obedience training for hog-tying the instructor. These dogs here are highly trained. The Pipster has spent her childhood in the presence of an old man who was crippled. This is probably the first time she's ever been to a park."

"Details, details, they can all be worked out. I was a South Valley girl with poor grammar skills and look at me now."

"B., we're talking about a dog here."

"I don't think it's fair of you to underestimate her like that. This could be her dream. Is it fair to deny her when the patron saint of dogs had obviously sent us here at just the right moment?" B. put her hands on her hips and stared hard at Chris.

"Far be it for me to trod on the tail of greatness. If she can do the commands, I'll stand by her."

"Deal."

They came back to Lola, who asked, "Are you two a couple?"

Chris laughed. "No, she's my best friend and we're roommates at the moment. We'd make really bad partners."

"So the deal is if the Pipster can perform the basic commands then she can try out," B. said, once again eyeing her protégé.

"Okay, let's give it a whirl."

The Pipster was still playing with her ball in a complicated series of soccer-like moves.

Lola called, "Pipster, come."

The dog grabbed her ball and came to Lola.

"Fluke," Chris said.

"We'll see," B. replied.

"Sit."

The Pipster sat perfectly, gazing up at Lola for the next command.

"Down."

The Pipster lay down.

"Stay," Lola instructed. She walked fifteen paces away and then turned around. "Come."

The Pipster ran to her.

Chris looked at B., who was beaming. It was at this moment Chris knew her entire life was going to revolve around a tennis ball. Thank goodness the eye candy was gorgeous.

Lola patted the dog on the head. "Let's try roll over."

Pippy obliged.

"Play dead."

The Pipster rolled on her back and stuck all four feet up in the air.

"That does it. Aliens have abducted our dog," Chris said.

B. got teary. "She's a genius."

"Oh, no," Chris said.

"Practice is Sunday morning at ten sharp."

"We'll be there," B. said.

B. let the Pipster sit on her lap while Chris drove the Lexus home. The Pipster drooled on the window and furred up B.'s swanky suit. B. didn't care. It was love, Chris thought. The two most important things in B.'s life were her car and her clothes. The Pipster had messed both of them up and B. didn't care. Chris had never seen B. look happier.

Chapter Ten

Several weeks had passed and B., despite her new love affair with Pippy, was in trouble. Diane found out about Jordan's cell phone and was threatening a restraining order. B. was indignant and then she was despondent. Chris had spent another night mopping up B.'s tears.

Luce had returned from Arizona. Chris was breathing easier. Luce was her rock and she felt unmoored when she was away.

Luce had stayed longer than she planned, well into June, hooking up with some other artists for a retreat in Prescott. "You should have seen this house," she told Chris. "We drank wine around the firepit at night, hiked all day, talked about art. I made some good sketches for future projects."

They were on a blanket in the park waiting for the Pipster's first game to start. The cottonwood trees in the park were shedding their white fluffy seeds. It look like it was snowing in June as the breeze caught the cotton ball clusters taking them to places unknown.

Luce took off her sandals. She'd painted her toenails turquoise and her middle toe had a toe ring on it.

"Do those things feel funny?" Chris asked, thinking how hip Luce always seemed. Today she was wearing a long purple skirt and a white embroidered linen shirt.

"No, it doesn't. I traded a small stained-glass piece with this nice man who makes jewelry. Look at this," she said, pulling the ring off.

The inside was inscribed, *Live the Dream*.

"Hey, that's cool." Chris handed it back to her.

"I thought so. Feet need dreams too."

Chris laughed.

"Now, what exactly have you gotten us into?" Luce said, pointing to the playing field.

"It's called fly ball. The Pipster is very good at it."

"I see that."

Lola, the coach, was throwing practice balls. The Pipster was hogging the scene much to the consternation of the other "parents."

"I think B. may have gone a little overboard." Chris pointed to B.'s and the Pipster's matching black starter outfits. B. had the Pipster's name embroidered on the back of hers. The outfit had side snaps so it could be pulled off at start time.

"It's cute. I had no idea they had things like that for dogs."

"Oh, you'd be surprised." Chris remembered with some hostility about being forced to go shopping with B. to find these cute outfits.

"I'm sensing you have a problem with this."

"Luce, she's a dog. Everyone seems to be forgetting that." Chris found herself getting just a bit edgy with the whole affair.

"But she has a loving nature and she's helping to heal B.'s broken heart."

"Okay, that's a good thing," Chris conceded, thinking it beat having a depressed roommate.

Jude, the stunning butch from the book club fiasco, joined them.

"Hello there, come sit," Luce said, patting the blanket.

"Thanks. B. invited me to come see Pippy play ball," Jude said.

Chris checked her out. She was well-dressed in khaki shorts and a white polo that accented her olive skin. She wore expensive Nike runners and equally expensive Oakley shades. She was perfect for B. B. was into curb appeal. Jude had it.

The game started and the Pipster was sure-footed, confident, well-behaved and fast. Chris was still entertaining the idea that aliens had abducted the real Pipster and replaced her with a model version, a prototype of the perfect dog.

During the first half of the game Jude did nothing but stare at B. Chris nudged Luce. "She's got it bad."

Luce smiled and nodded.

"I do," Jude said, turning her attention to them.

"Does B. know?" Luce asked.

"Yes. We've talked. She's still healing. I respect that. I don't want to be a rebound case."

All eyes returned to the game as B. screamed with joy at the Pipster's performance.

"Are you going to wait?" Chris asked.

"Damn right."

"Good for you, Jude," Luce said.

Chris could tell that Luce liked Jude. There wasn't much not to like—she was smart, good-looking and sweet.

"I think she's the most amazing woman I've ever met. She's driven yet sensitive, competitive and competent," Jude said.

B. sounded a bit like a brochure, Chris thought, but infatuation could do that. "Not to mention her physical accoutrements."

"I fall down on my knees in praise of the Goddess."

Chris laughed. "You're all right, sister."

There was much jocularity around the team upon their trouncing of the competition. B. brought the Pipster over. She lit up when she saw Jude. The Pipster licked Chris's face and then collapsed onto the blanket in complete exhaustion.

"Isn't she precious," Luce said, leaning over and scratching her ears.

"She's in heaven," Chris said.

"I think someone else is as well," Luce replied.

B. was hugging Jude and cooing over the fact that she'd made time to come to the game.

"They look good together," Chris commented, thinking Jude's handsome butchness complemented B.'s femininity. Physically, they were made for each other.

"So I'm thinking the book club wasn't a wash after all," Luce said.

"Except that Jude has those two creepy friends."

"Perhaps they're well-meaning friends that got caught up in a bad moment."

Chris smirked. "Boy, talk about good spin."

Luce smiled sweetly.

"So what's next on our dating quest?"

"Amadeus is hooking up with the community center."

"What will we do there?"

"Whatever they want us to. That's the nature of volunteer work," Luce replied.

"The unplanned makes me nervous," Chris said. She patted the Pipster's head. She was snoring.

"I know, but it's important that we stretch our horizons," Luce said. She took Chris's hand. "It'll be fine. Besides I think it's a positive thing that Amadeus is initiating a dating activity."

"You're right. We had a hard time getting her to come along to the book club."

"My thoughts exactly."

"Hey, girls, let's get some lunch at the Zoo and celebrate the Pipster's first, very successful game," B. said.

"What about the Pipster? It's too hot to leave her in the car. I can take her home," Chris offered.

"It's her celebration. She can have a burger," B. said, swishing Chris's concerns away with her hand.

The Pipster woke and went over to B. and sat next to her. *The dog knows who butters her bread*, Chris thought wryly.

"Jude, are you coming with?" Luce said, helping Chris fold up the quilt.

"Of course she is," B. answered, linking her arm through Jude's.

"I'll ride with Luce," Chris said.

They followed B. and Jude out of the parking lot. Chris could tell they were talking.

"They seem to really like each other," Luce said.

Luce had traded in her old truck for this huge green Ram Charger. Chris wondered what spurred the change.

"They do. Jude sure is a looker."

"Sounds like you like her too," Luce said.

"Come on, she's all over B."

Chris's cell phone rang. It was B.

"I forgot to tell you I invited Lola."

"You what?"

"She likes you. What's wrong with a group lunch? I thought that's what this is all about—finding the love of your life," B. replied.

"Have you found yours?"

"I'm not at liberty to say."

"I bet. 'Bye." Chris clicked off.

"What was that about?" Luce asked as they drove up Central.

"B. thinks the Pipster's coach, Lola, has the hots for me."

"Does she?"

"Beats me." Chris changed the subject. "What's with the new wheels?"

"I decided holding on to that truck was sentimental. I was keeping up my unhealthy attachment to Claire. So I bought this new beauty." She patted the dashboard affectionately. "This is a good rig for the business and I think she looks good on me."

"She does. What's her name?" Chris asked. Luce always named her vehicles. Doris the Dodge was the last one. Luce believed in the importance of developing a personal relationship with her vehicle. It made for good karma.

"Her name is Randy."

"Randy the Ram Charger."

"Precisely."

They passed through the University District. The Frontier Restaurant was packed with college students. The line trailed out the door and down the block. It was the place to meet and be seen. Chris had spent a good portion of her youth doing the same thing. The food was good and it was cheap. Breakfast, lunch or dinner could lead to the bedroom.

"Was it hard to let Doris go?"

"Kind of, but I found her a good home. I donated her to Casa Esperanza, the hospice."

"That's a neat thing to do."

They reached the Zoo. The parking lot was nearly full. Amadeus would be happy. A full restaurant was a profitable one. B. and Jude parked two spaces over.

"Good crowd," B. said. She pulled dark glasses from her purse, the kind old people with sun-sensitive eyes wear. Then she opened the trunk and pulled out an elaborate leather harness. "Come here, Pippy."

"She can't come in," Chris said.

"Of course she can. Don't be a petaphobic. She's my escort. I've been taking her everywhere. She's very well-behaved. Aren't you, Pippy?"

The Pipster slipped into her harness easily. Obviously, she was well-versed in this procedure, Chris concluded.

"B., don't tell me you've got her being a guide dog for the blind?" Luce said.

"Well, of course. She's good at it. Lead on, Pippy."

B. took hold of the harness and the dog went straight for the door, even stopping when a car pulled out of the drive.

"She is good at it," Chris said. She could see Lola waiting for them at the front door.

"This is just wrong," Luce said. "It's a complete charade."

"I know, but it's keeping her mind off Diane," Chris said.

Amadeus was not pleased with the dog in the restaurant.

"Will you just relax? No one will notice. Just get Rose to fix her a hamburger—no mayo and no lettuce. She doesn't like veggies," B. instructed.

Amadeus insisted they take a table at the back. It was a large round table near the kitchen. "I can't believe you," she said, throwing her hands up in the air. "You're hopeless."

"She secretly loves me," B. replied.

"Right. You better hope the health inspector never gets hold of this or you're toast," Chris said, taking a seat.

"Lola, you sit next to me with Jude here. And Luce, you sit over there," B. said.

"What for?" Chris said, sliding over.

"The purpose of conversation," B. replied.

Everyone settled in. Amadeus came to take their order.

"Oh, my, the big lady herself," Chris said.

Amadeus gave her a dirty look. "I don't want my staff getting wind of this," she said, pointing to B. and the dog at her feet.

"She's not doing anything. This is her treat for being a star player," B. said.

"She did play extremely well for her first official game," Lola said.

Amadeus raised an eyebrow and looked at B. This was the

Germanic expression for letting B. know she'd forgotten her manners.

"Amadeus, meet Lola Vasquez. She's Pippy's coach on the fly ball team," B. said.

"Charmed," Amadeus said, extending her hand.

Lola flushed when she took it. "The pleasure is mine."

Amadeus handed out the menus. "I'll be back shortly."

"Amadeus, is Midge working?" Chris asked.

"No, she left early—something about doorknobs."

"Speaking of Midge, wait until you see the house we found her," B. said. She was beaming, which meant big money.

"You found her a house already?" Chris said. She knew Midge was working with B. to find a house but she didn't know they'd gotten started already. Of course, B. never wasted a business opportunity.

"Oh, my God, it's absolutely perfect—Northeast Heights, cute but not overly small."

"I can't believe you didn't tell me."

"She just closed last Friday. She's having her stuff moved out of storage on Monday. She doesn't waste any time. I like that."

"You two are starting to act like a couple," Luce said.

"We are not!" they said in unison.

"So now, why is it that you two live together?" Lola asked.

"B. was between residences and I'd thrown out my girlfriend for sleeping with her rock-climbing instructor," Chris replied with a shrug.

"I see," Lola said as she picked up her menu.

"I'm not bitter or anything." She opened her own menu. She was thinking cheese enchiladas sounded good.

"Lola, what do you do other than coach fly ball?" Luce asked.

"I'm a molecular scientist at Sandia Labs," Lola said, looking up from her menu.

Jude was consulting with B. about something on the menu. Chris pretended to be overly interested in her menu while she eavesdropped on the Luce and Lola interchange. It was out of character for Luce to be so forward.

"I guess we won't be inquiring into that line of work. I'm sure I wouldn't understand the first thing about the vocabulary," Luce said.

"It's actually quite dull. Fly ball and the dogs are my passion."

"It sure has turned the Pipster around," Chris said. "Lola is great with the dogs."

"Thanks, Chris," Lola said, staring at her longer than was necessary.

"B. tells me that you rescued the Pipster."

"Well, I don't know about that. I just didn't want her put down because she couldn't be placed. I don't think being homeless warrants a death sentence."

"That's a rescue to me and it's very admirable." Lola touched Chris's hand.

Chris felt the heat and returned Lola's gaze. Her nether regions jumped in anticipation.

"Lola, are you in a relationship?" Luce asked. She set her menu down and stared intently at her.

"Not at the moment. I haven't been serious about anyone in a while, but it's not like I couldn't be enticed."

Amadeus came back with a tray laden with glasses of water and a huge platter of cheese, meats and crackers. "Have you decided?"

"I think so," Chris replied. She hoped the ordering process would dispel the obvious animosity between Luce and Lola.

"B., would you like to start?" Amadeus asked. She didn't have an order pad but rather committed their selections to memory. Her staff strove for the same goal. Chris admired the grace and expertise of this practice. It was completely highbrow.

"We'll have the Reuben sandwich, borscht and a small garden salad with blue cheese dressing."

"We?" Amadeus raised an eyebrow.

"Jude and I," B. said, blushing slightly.

For not being a couple they were certainly behaving like one, Chris noted.

Jude explained. "B. knows the menu so well—I figured she'd make the best choice."

"I see," Amadeus replied. "To drink?"

"Iced tea for both," B. replied.

"Chris?"

"Cheese enchiladas and a Corona."

"I'll have the same thing," Lola said.

"Exactly?"

"Yes, please."

"Luce?"

"Cheese fondue and a garden salad with a glass of chardonnay."

"Perfect." Amadeus went back to the kitchen.

"So, Luce, what do you do?" Lola asked.

Luce smiled. "I'm a stained-glass artist."

Chris couldn't tell if Lola thought Luce was competition or if she was just curious. She supposed Lola was trying to figure out how they all fit together. Luce wasn't behaving like herself at all. It was as if Luce was jealous or afraid that Lola was going to make a move. Chris could feel the distant twinge between her legs. She drowned it out with reasonable talk. She knew Lola was not the love of her life come calling. She thought of the story about how Alice B. Toklas heard ringing in her ears whenever she met a genius. They rang for Gertrude Stein. Chris had a similar experience with love. Her ears didn't ring but she felt an electrical charge course through her veins and set on one destination: her heart. She felt this with her very first love and with Claire. The rest of her lovers were raging hormones and had more to do with below the waist than her ventricles.

"Do you make church windows?" Lola asked politely.

Luce laughed. They couldn't be more different, Chris

thought. The artist and the scientist trying to find common ground.

"No, I do mostly abstracts for corporate offices, galleries and art fairs," Luce explained.

Amadeus brought the Pipster's hamburger. She must have smelled it because she was sitting at attention by B.'s side. "I beg you, please be discreet."

"Angus beef." B. sniffed it discerningly.

Amadeus rolled her eyes.

B. snapped open her cloth napkin and tied it around the Pipster's neck. The dog didn't protest, confirming Chris's suspicion that this wasn't a new practice. B. cut the beef patty into bite-sized pieces, which she fed to the Pipster right off the fork. They all stared. The dog ate with manners and finesse. "What?" she asked, noticing her audience.

"That's amazing. You should be a trainer," Lola said.

"That's disgusting," Amadeus said. She pulled another place setting off an empty table, replacing the one B. had used.

"This is definitely over the top," Luce whispered to Chris.

Chris smiled. "She's the kid B. always wanted and—"

"I know, it keeps her mind off Diane."

"What do you mean? That dog should be on television," Jude said.

Just then Amadeus's cell phone rang. She pulled it out of her trouser pocket. "Yes, hold on." She handed the phone to Chris. "It's Midge. She wants to talk to you."

"There you are. I've been trying to get ahold of you all morning. I suppose you left your cell phone somewhere."

Chris was notorious for not having it with her. Maybe it was something Freudian, like she didn't really want to be that connected. "I left my cell phone in my work satchel."

"I figured as much."

"Hey, congratulations on the new house." Chris looked over at B., who was smiling.

"It's a great house. It's out of your post office. Just off Carlyle Street, on Solano."

"That's nice in there."

"I was lucky to get it. B.'s a simply amazing Realtor once you get past her whirling dervish behavior."

Chris laughed. "Consider it a Godsend that it was over quickly."

This time Midge laughed. "The reason I called was that I wanted to ask you if you thought having a housewarming party and inviting the other gals was a good idea."

"That sounds great."

"Would you feel comfortable inviting them while you've got them all there?"

"Of course, Midge. Hold on." She covered the receiver with her palm. "Ladies, how about a house party at Midge's new place?"

"Fantastic. It's been ages since we've had one," B. said.

"It's a go, Midge."

"Great, I was thinking next Saturday night. I'll be moved in by then."

"Perfect. I'll help."

"I was counting on it."

"I'm there." Chris clicked off and handed the phone back to Amadeus.

Two servers brought the food out. Pippy was snoring under the table. Chris looked at her friends and decided this was better than sleeping around. She'd remind herself of that if Lola ever made a pass at her. She bit into her cheese enchiladas. They were fabulous.

Chapter Eleven

The following Saturday, Chris cruised down Solano Street carefully studying the addresses. As a mailman following directions, knowing which side of the street the even and odd addresses were on came as second nature. The neighborhood was comprised of older adobe homes with a few sprawling ranch houses sprinkled in. There were large trees and mostly xeriscaped yards with a few bluegrass lawns that their owners were paying through the nose for. Water was a luxury of a bygone era for people who had lived in the Midwest and then retired to a milder climate. The Southwest was full of them. These people loved their grass and couldn't quit the habit. *You couldn't pay me to get behind a mower*, she thought.

Midge's house sat dead center in the block. The front yard was filled with a wide variety of low-water-use plants; bristle bush, purple sage and red salvias along with several large yuccas gave the yard the look of a wild desert oasis nestled in the city. It had to have been professionally done. A path wound through the landscape and up to the covered front porch which ran around the side of the house as well. The porch had a red brick floor and heavy, rough-hewn support poles. Wooden benches rested against the adobe walls. Chris stood marveling. B. was right. The place was gorgeous.

Midge must have heard her motorcycle pull up. She came out the screen door. "You like it?"

"Midge, this place is amazing."

"The man who built it was a fanatic about authenticity. Wait until you see the inside."

"Let me guess—kiva fireplace, beamed ceilings, tile, and inset bookcases and trinket nooks."

"You got it. I love the Southwest style."

Midge gave Chris a tour, explaining that the man who built the house worked for the Desert Botanical Gardens in Phoenix. He was from back East and adored the desert. He couldn't take the heat and massive growth Phoenix was experiencing, though, so he opted for New Mexico for his retirement. "He poured his soul into this house."

"How do you know all this?" Chris asked.

"B. got all this info from the man's last living relative, his sister. She wanted to find just the right buyer."

"Good grief, that woman would walk over hot coals if it meant selling a house." Chris touched one of the whitewashed walls. "Is this true adobe?"

"Yes. I did appreciate the history lesson, but I would have bought the house anyway. Come on, let's get a cocktail and I can show you what I did to the kitchen. I took the liberty of inviting the very attractive carpenter who did the work to the party and she's bringing a friend."

"More participants increase our odds."

"I never took you for a numbers girl."

"I'm not good with a checkbook. Did you get your hair high-lighted?" Chris noticed Midge's tasteful outfit, a dark green silk blouse and a pair of black, pin-striped trousers and a gold vest.

"I did. What do you think?"

"It looks great." Midge's red hair, now glowing with blond highlights, complemented her outfit. "You sort of match."

"I planned that." Midge led her into the modified kitchen.

"I'm no good at clothes. B. tried to take me shopping and it was a disaster."

"I should take you to Solegros. We could find you something there. I'm sure of it."

"You mean something other than jeans and a T-shirt?" She glanced down at her Levi's.

"They work on you. Black jeans and a white shirt are classic," Midge said.

Chris could tell she was being diplomatic. "You're sweet."

Chris looked around the modified kitchen. The countertops and cabinets were lowered. The kitchen island with its stainless steel top and swivel-back chairs were all lowered. Chris felt like she was Alice in Wonderland as she outgrew the house. Soon her overgrown arms and legs would be sticking out the windows and doors.

"What do you think?"

"It's either I got taller or you made everything shorter."

"Not too much shorter, I hope. Here, stand by the island and put your hands on it."

Chris complied. It wasn't too low. "It's like the perfect compromise."

"Great. I didn't want everything so low that it would be uncomfortable for regular people, but it needed it to be practical for me."

"How did you do it?"

"The carpenter I told you about, Gabriela, essentially modified everything. She used to work for California Closets before going out on her own. She's had a lot of practice doing custom work. She changed out all the doors too."

"The door handles are lower," Chris said, looking at them.

"Yes, Gabriela is an amazing woman."

"And quick too." She remembered that Midge had mentioned doorknobs only last weekend. She obviously wanted it done for the party.

"The deadlines are a useful tool when dealing with tradespeople." Midge pulled two Coronas and a small bowl of fresh-cut limes from what looked like a cabinet.

"Is that a fridge?" Chris asked, incredulous that such a thing existed.

"It is." Midge opened the bottles.

Chris opened the fridge and peered inside.

"The freezer is right below it."

Chris pulled it open. "Okay, this is really cool."

"Come on, let's go sit on the back veranda and sip these," Midge said, picking up the beers.

"What about the snack trays?"

"They can wait. We've still got time. The shrimp needs to thaw before we make the hors d'oeurvres."

Chris nodded. She'd volunteered to help Midge with the food for the party. Amadeus was bringing a spiral ham. Luce had finished the stained-glass piece of the orange daylilies commemorating the day B. lost her cell phone in the pond and the formation of the Date Night Club. It was the perfect housewarming gift. Chris had bought four red chili ristras to hang from the veranda. Luce was bringing them because they wouldn't fit on Chris's bike.

B. managed through the sister to get photographs and construction notes from the man who'd built the house. She'd put together a scrapbook as a mini-history of the house. B. couldn't wait to show Midge.

Chris eased back into one of the chaise lounges lined up on

the covered back veranda. She noticed there were exactly six. She wondered if there would someday be twelve if everyone hooked up.

Chris said, "Did Luce tell you that we're all going to the Fourth of July pride picnic for the community center?"

"Yes. Amadeus and I volunteered as cooks. You and Luce are beer tenders and B. is doing tickets. I think it's a perfect activity for our Date Night Club community adventure."

Chris suddenly panicked. "This makes me nervous. I'd envisioned sort of easing into this thing."

Midge reached over and touched her hand. "You'll be serving beer to people who are getting sloshed. How difficult can that be?"

"I guess you're right." Chris sipped her Corona. She looked out at the lovely backyard. It had the same tasteful artistry of the front. A set of Joshua trees blocked the view of the neighbor's house and a giant mulberry tree served as another privacy screen. This gave the yard the illusion of being out in the middle of nowhere. There was the occasional space where the adobe wall peeked through the abundant foliage, subtly reminding her that it was indeed a city yard. Chris and Midge sat silently, taking in the twilight as it bathed the evening in a watercolor pink. It was shattered with the arrival of B. and Jude. Chris controlled a snicker. For not dating they sure spent a lot of time together.

Midge must have caught it as well. "Oh, it's the uncouple."

Chris chuckled.

"What are you two doing? Where are the party trays? I knew I should've had this catered," B. said, placing her hands on her hips.

"B., relax. I've got everything prepped. All we have to do is assemble. The brioches will get soggy if done too far ahead of time. The shrimp is still thawing. The smoked salmon and caviar are already on trays. All is well," Midge said.

B. let out a sigh. "I suppose you're right."

"I'll get the Champagne on ice," Jude said.

"I'll help," B. said.

"I see Gabriela got you fixed up. The house looks fabulous," Jude said.

"She did. She's coming tonight," Midge replied.

"So I heard, and bringing a hot date with her," Jude said.

"We'll be in the kitchen," B. said, taking Jude's hand.

"I think we'd better get started," Midge said, getting up.

"B. has the uncanny ability to explode serenity," Chris said, following Midge into the house.

"B., what did you do with the Pipster?" She couldn't imagine she'd leave her home.

"She's in here waiting for you," B. said. She emptied the bags of ice into a large silver bucket. Jude followed behind her, sticking the Champagne bottles in.

The Pipster, sitting at attention in the center of the kitchen, was dressed in a black silk tuxedo with a plaited white dress shirt and black tie.

"At least I didn't have to help shop for this one. It was mail order," Chris said.

"She's absolutely darling," Midge said. She patted her on the head and when the Pipster licked her hand, Midge rewarded her with a biscuit. She really liked Midge.

Chris suspected it was because she was the only person who didn't appear to be a giant.

"Now, go get Midge your hostess gift," B. instructed.

The Pipster cocked her head.

"Oh, I'm sorry. Get the present."

The Pipster happily trotted off.

"Her language coach keeps getting on me about using interchangeable words. Pippy's not at that level yet," B. said.

"She has a language coach," Chris said. *Now, I've seen everything*, she thought.

"Well, of course. Dogs normally develop a vocabulary of one hundred and fifty words. I intend to stretch her horizons."

"Of course," Chris said, rolling her eyes.

"I think B. has done wonders with Pippy," Jude said, smiling widely at B.

Chris noticed B.'s face color slightly. They both looked happy and made a stunning couple. B. had trimmed her hair to shoulder length and given it a body wave, creating a soft look around her high cheekbones. She'd purchased some new blouses that showed off her best features and changed the color of her lipstick. Chris suspected that Jude's presence had brought out B.'s more feminine side. She wondered when the uncouple would admit their attraction. If B. changed her hair, her clothes and her lipstick, it was serious.

The Pipster came back into the room carrying a bouquet of white calla lilies tied up tightly with a yellow ribbon so that she could pick them up using her mouth. *B. thinks of everything*, Chris mused.

"How sweet," Midge said, taking the flowers from the dog.

"She's been practicing that trick all morning," B. said. She pulled a biscuit from her pocket. "High five."

The Pipster jumped up and lay one paw on B.'s outstretched palm. B. gave her the treat.

"That dog is simply amazing," Midge said.

The doorbell rang. Midge and Pippy went to answer it. It was Amadeus. She was decked out in copper-colored dress suit. It went well with her blue eyes and red hair, Chris thought. She looked like a twenty-first-century Amazon.

"Amadeus, you look great," B. said. She stroked the lapel of the jacket. "Where did you get it?"

Amadeus smiled coyly. "Not anywhere around here."

"Damn it." B. eyed the suit and pouted.

"I don't want you having another one made for you-know-who," Amadeus said, pointing at the Pipster.

"I would, too," B. said, laughing. "Do you like her tuxedo?"

"It's absurd."

Midge gave her a look.

"I mean, she carries it well," Amadeus said. "Now, Chris, can you help me get some stuff out of the car."

"Speaking of cars, did the insurance company finally sort out your claim?" Chris asked. She hadn't run into Shirley since she bashed Amadeus's car windows with the rolling pin. Just as well, she thought.

"They did. I'm free of that awful rental Crown Vic."

Chris followed Amadeus outside. She sensed something was up. "Nice car," she said. It was a crème-colored Mercedes with a brown leather interior. It fairly breathed luxury and speed.

"What do you think?" Amadeus asked as she popped open the trunk.

"It's a step up. Perhaps losing the Beemer has a silver lining," Chris ran a finger down the fender.

Amadeus grunted. "Not so sure about that. Look, do you think this thing between B. and Jude is good?"

"Sure, why not?"

Amadeus took out the carefully covered ham and handed it to Chris. It was heavy. She hoped this would be a short conversation.

"I don't know."

"Do you have a bad vibe about it?" Chris asked, her biceps quivering.

"I'm concerned that B. is still holding out for Diane and stringing Jude along."

"Jude's a big girl."

Amadeus grabbed a shopping bag and closed the trunk. "I don't want you to say anything, but I saw Diane out last night with another woman."

"You did? It was probably just a friend." Chris suddenly felt weak. If B. got ahold of this, life would be a misery.

"On the dance floor."

111

"Oh, God."

"I don't think even He can help. I haven't decided whether to tell B. or keep it to myself. I want your advice."

"You must be desperate."

"I am."

Chris laughed nervously. "I think B. is falling in love with Jude. She'll find out one way or another. There'll be a slew of tears and then she'll move on. Realistically, Jude is a better match than Diane," she said, faking a calmness she didn't possess.

Amadeus furrowed her brow. "I had no idea you were so intuitive."

"It's from hanging around with Midge. Can we go inside now? This ham is heavy."

"Oh, yes. I'm sorry."

"Speaking of dating, any women on your horizon?" Chris asked as they made their way to the house.

"I'm still tentative."

"Because you just got your new car."

Amadeus chuckled. This was unusual for her. "Maybe you're getting a little too intuitive."

"Not all dykes are car-beaters."

"I hope not," Amadeus said, taking a wistful, longing look at her new Mercedes.

"Maybe Date Night Club should go to a car show to find you a babe," Chris said.

"Now, that's a good idea."

As a friend, Amadeus would forever be an enigma, Chris thought. She saw Luce's truck coming down the street. She'd be out for another load. She dropped the ham off in the kitchen where Jude, B. and Midge were drinking Champagne and making the shrimp cocktails.

"I'll be right back. Luce is here," Chris told Midge.

Luce was in the bed of the pickup carefully uncrating her work of art. She'd used old wooden pallets and padded them with heavy blankets purchased long ago from a moving company that had gone out of business.

"Thank you," Luce said, taking Chris's hand and hopping down to the ground. "I just wanted to get it unwrapped."

Chris stared at her.

"What?" Luce asked. She smoothed out her powder blue blazer. It had red, green and purple stars on it.

"You look like a rock star."

"I do, don't I? I found it at the Buffalo Exchange."

"You look great." Chris hugged her. Not only did she look good but she smelled good—like a swirling mix of citrus and flowers—as if she'd walked through paradise and only just arrived in the city. Chris held her longer than was necessary but Luce didn't seem to mind. They were doing that more now. Chris refused to let her mind run with it, yet she found her body craving the attention. She figured this was merely a sign of recent deprivation.

"I bought you a present."

"Oh, really?" Chris said, releasing her.

Luce smiled coyly. She went to the front seat of the truck and pulled out a velvet blazer and a white ruffled blouse. "Here, try it on."

"Is it my party outfit?" Chris put the blouse over her T-shirt and then slipped on the blazer. Luce pulled a pair of yellow-tinted round spectacles from the breast pocket. Chris put them on.

"Fabulous. Now we both look like rock stars," Luce said.

Chris looked at her reflection of the truck's window. "I actually look hip."

"You do. Come on. Let's get Midge's present inside."

They maneuvered the three-foot-by-two-foot glass piece out of the truck bed and up to the front porch. Luce had framed it in oak with a stand.

Midge was ecstatic when she saw it. "It's the orange daylilies from Chris's yard."

Chris was sick of lifting heavy things—first the ham and now the art. She curbed the impulse to scream.

Midge must have noticed. "For goodness' sake, put it down. Thank you, Luce. It's lovely."

"I got you some ristras for the veranda," Chris said. "I'll be right back." She ran to Luce's truck and returned with the ristras.

"These are lovely."

They were almost as tall as Midge. Amadeus took them. "I'll put them out back."

"You changed," Midge noted, eyeing Chris's shirt.

"I got hip in the driveway."

"I like it," Midge said, handing her a glass of Champagne.

"Let's get stinking drunk tonight," Chris said.

"But no riding your bike," Midge said.

"I'll go with Luce, and you have to be careful crawling to your bedroom."

"Deal."

"Let's take our drinks out back," Midge said.

Luce, Chris and Midge sat on the back veranda watching the sky turning from reddish pink to an inky blue with a waning crescent moon coming into view.

"The sky here is simply amazing," Midge said, leaning back in her chaise lounge.

"That's one of the things I like best about summer. The sun sets later so I'm off work and I can enjoy it," Chris said.

"I like summer because I don't have to wear socks all the time," Luce said. She wiggled her toes.

They heard shouting from the kitchen.

"What the hell?" Midge said.

Since they were outside that left B., Jude and Amadeus in the kitchen.

"I wonder if Amadeus and B. are going at it," Chris said.

"I don't think so," Luce said. "It sounds like B. and Diane."

"You didn't invite Diane, did you?" Chris asked Midge.

"I don't even know Diane. I invited Gabriela and her date."

"Is her girlfriend blond, pretty and has a little girl?" Chris asked, putting together what Amadeus had told her and what was going on in the kitchen.

Midge looked at her queerly.

"What are you getting at?" Luce asked.

"I think—" She was cut off by Amadeus coming out the back door.

They could hear B. yelling, "You could have told me that you're dating someone."

"We're not together. I don't have to report to you," Diane yelled back.

"Chris, we need backup," Amadeus said, poking her head out the screen door.

"Oh, my, our worse fears are realized," Chris said, hopping up. She flew into the kitchen where B. and Diane were having a standoff.

Jude stood next to B., and Diane's new girlfriend, Gabriela, was holding Diane's hand. She was a tall, Hispanic woman with her long black hair pulled back. She had full lips, high cheekbones and green eyes. She was clearly gorgeous and this added to B.'s ire. Not to mention she wore a tailored olive rayon suit that made her look even more professional than B. The competition had outdone her and B. wasn't going to take this lying down.

The Pipster was barking, Chris supposed in defense of B. The cacophony was horrendous. Chris stuck her fingers in her mouth and did her best ballfield whistle.

Pippy stopped barking and sat at attention. "Good girl," she patted her head.

B. and Diane stopped bickering. They all stared at Chris.

"B., Diane is correct. She's free to date whomever she pleases. It's not Gabriela's fault Diane is her date. She didn't know. Nor did Midge intend for this to happen."

"That doesn't excuse it," B. replied.

115

Chris gave her the behave-or-you-won't-get-a treat look that she'd been practicing with the Pipster. It had proved effective, not only with the dog but also with some of her coworkers. It worked on B., perhaps because of her symbiotic relationship with Pippy.

"B., you're in love with Jude, so pretending to pine over Diane is prevarication at its utmost," Amadeus said.

They all turned to stare at her. She was making tiny ham sandwiches and stacking them neatly on a silver platter. "What? Is being truthful that out of line? Buck up."

Chris laughed. "I love when you do Germanic Americana."

B. turned beet red. "That is not your place," she said to Amadeus.

Amadeus shrugged. "I never took you for a coward."

This sent B. into overdrive. "I'm not a coward. Of course I love Jude. I just don't like surprises. Diane has moved on and so have I." She took Jude's hand and kissed it.

Luce and Midge were standing in the doorway, checking to see if it was safe to come inside. Luce clapped, the rest followed. B. outdid herself and curtseyed. She gave Diane a hug and congratulated her on her good taste.

"Okay, now that we've solved that problem, let's have a toast and eat. I'm famished," Chris said.

B. wrapped her arms around Jude, who was clearly still trying to regain her composure. "Is this all right with you?"

Jude nodded.

Chapter Twelve

"At least we have one success from Date Night Club," Chris said. They were parked out front of her house after the party. Luce had driven her home. Both B.'s Lexus and Jude's red Mini-Cooper were parked in the driveway. The house was dark. It was after midnight, which meant either they were sleeping or having sex.

"Perhaps you should stay with me tonight," Luce suggested.

"That works for me. We can go to breakfast tomorrow at the Range."

"Sometimes I wonder if you come to see me or to be close to your favorite restaurant."

Chris feigned hurt. "It's only you."

Luce flipped a U-turn and headed toward the freeway.

"I'm glad B. is finally off Diane. It seems too futile to hang on to someone who's long gone. I know she misses Jordan, but maybe now Diane will let her see the kid."

Luce laughed. She looked over her shoulder to check for traffic and then merged onto the freeway.

"What? I mean, Diane wouldn't let her see Jordan because she was afraid B. would use the kid to worm her way back into Diane's life. That's a pretty astute assessment of B."

"No, not that. I was laughing about how we think B. held on so long, and look at the two of us."

Chris stared out the window at the billboards as they whizzed by. She thought for a moment. "We've improved."

"In what way?" Luce asked. She exited at Tramway.

Chris preferred going the back way. The twinkling lights of the houses against the black monolith of the Sandia Mountains always seemed homey and reassuring, like those miniature light-up villages that people put up on their coffee tables at Christmastime.

"Well . . ." Chris stumbled. "You bought a new truck and I'm no longer fucking imbeciles."

Luce patted the dash of her truck.

"See," Chris said.

"You're right. I think about Claire a lot less since we've started our quest."

"I think we're all doing better. Amadeus might need a push."

"Why?"

"She's got a new car and she's definitely suffering from posttraumatic rolling pin syndrome. I told her all lesbians aren't carbeaters."

Luce laughed. "You're horrible."

"That's why you love me."

"I do," Luce said. She patted Chris's hand and then took hold of it. Neither of them said anything. Chris's heart pounded and she tried hard not to think anything other than friendship.

The next morning Chris awoke to find Luce sitting on the edge of the bed holding a steaming cup of black coffee. Chris rubbed her eyes and tried to orient herself. Her neck was kinked from having slept with no pillows, but at least her feet were warm. She managed to untangle herself from the sheets and sat up.

"Do you always sleep upside down?" Luce handed her the cup of coffee.

"No. I had this freaky dream."

"Do tell." Luce looked the picture of interest.

"I don't know if I should. It's kind of embarrassing." Chris sipped her coffee. The room was bathed in a purple glow from the batik curtains. The guest room had a low ceiling, and Chris always felt that she was staying in a room straight out of *The Hobbit*.

"It's only a dream. They simply give us a window to our subconscious."

"That's just it."

"Come on. Now you've got me really curious."

"You have to promise not to laugh."

"I would never."

"I dreamt that I was trapped in a giant vagina. The cervix was a trampoline and I was trying to jump high enough to scale the wall and crawl out." She waited for Luce's response.

Luce's red silk kimono had slipped off her left shoulder, revealing part of her collarbone. She flounced down on the bed and laughed hysterically. Chris wanted to kiss her.

She rolled on her side to look at Chris. "I'm sorry. I couldn't resist. I can't wait to tell B."

"You promised. I will never live it down. It has to stay right here."

Luce pouted. "It seems absolutely wicked not to share something so hysterical."

"Luce . . ."

"All right." She got up quickly, kissed Chris on the lips and said, "I promise. Now get showered and dressed. Midge and Amadeus insist we return for breakfast as there still Champagne and half a spiral ham left. I don't think they've been to bed. They were laughing quite heartily when it took Amadeus three attempts to say 'omelet.'"

"Oh, this'll be prime." Chris hopped up.

"I found you some shorts and a shirt. They're on the counter in the bathroom."

Once alone, Chris pondered Luce's sudden attentions. Had Luce been any other woman, Chris would have had her in bed by now. But Luce was different. Were these physical moments a fluke of their long friendship or something more? Luce had held her before. They'd spent the night in the same bed after Claire died. Chris held her while she cried and they both grieved, but it had never been sexual—on Luce's part, she conceded. She, on the other hand, thought Luce was sensual, soft and sexy. She would never openly admit these things to anyone. She barely allowed herself to.

By the time she had showered and dressed, her stomach and her brain were both tied up in knots. She found Luce out back on the patio watering giant pots of lavender and hanging baskets of white petunias. "The garden looks awesome," she said, pointing to the raised beds full of flowers and vegetables.

Luce smiled. "I love this time of year. In July all the hard work becomes manifest, and goodness knows, wheedling life from the desert is a triumph."

"You've done well."

"Thanks. B. called. She and Jude are meeting us for breakfast."

"I'd rather have breakfast alone with you at the Range."

Luce finished watering. "Me too, but we've got to be supportive or B. will take it the wrong way."

"Like we don't approve of something." Chris coiled up the hose for her.

"You never know."

"Would it be over the top if I did a Maypole dance around her and kissed Jude's feet for rescuing us all from the depths of B.'s burgeoning depression?"

"Yes. I forbid it."

"I'll control myself."

"Come on. I'm starving," Luce said, shutting the French doors.

Chris smiled as she got in the truck. Every day was an improvement on the last. It was a perfect sunny day, she was spending it with her best friends, and B. had gotten laid. God had surely saved them.

Chapter Thirteen

By the following Monday morning, Chris was trying to revive that feeling of euphoria she had felt driving into town with Luce. B. had been on cloud nine and gone MIA with Jude. The house seemed kind of dull but she'd talked to Luce later that night and gone to bed in a much better mood.

It was quickly evaporating as her coworker Gomez was screaming, "Fuck you, you stupid fucking fuck," at Sanchez, his floater.

"I do Advo on my day on your route, you stupid prick. You should do the same. You're nothing but a pussy."

Chris tried to temper the whole thing. "Gentlemen, may I remind you there are ladies present." This was the cue for all female personnel to step out of their cases and give a show of force. It worked. Mary, Pat, Rose and Delia stepped out and put their hands on their hips. The Postal Service was adamant about sexual harassment and the boys knew it.

"I meant you're a vagina," Sanchez replied. "That's a biological term."

George, the PFT that Chris had trained, stuck her head out of her case and looked completely mortified. It was always a shock for new hires in the beginning. The Post Office was not for the weak of heart.

Mary, a large black woman who was at least four inches taller than Sanchez, stared him down. "Boyfriend, why don't you turn that thong you're wearing around and relax that overeducated mouth of yours before I do it for you. You know that man doesn't have the testicular fortitude to carry half his route. You think the eunuch can do Advo too. He might break a sweat and ruin his pretty hairdo."

This brought a rash of laughter. Both Mary and Sanchez had long college careers but had opted for the postal salary, which was double that of a teaching job. Still, they couldn't help verbal repartee when it suited them. The Postal Service was full of overeducated misfits who'd found a place where being odd was considered the norm. That's what Chris liked best about it.

Chris's cell phone rang. It was B.

Gomez stepped toward Sanchez and the stare-down began.

"B., what's up? I'm kind in the middle of an altercation here," Chris said as she stepped between the two. Workplace violence was another postal no-no. If they so much as touched each other, they'd be fired, and it would take months and a mountain of paperwork for her to get their jobs back.

"Chris, I can't believe it. Diane called and I can see Jordan for the day and it's fine if Jude comes along."

"That's great, B. So what's wrong?" Chris knew B. didn't call to announce good news. It was only in a crisis that she made courtesy calls.

Gomez and Sanchez were dancing around her, arguing in low tones because she was on the phone.

"What makes you think something is wrong?"

"B., don't be coy. I'm short on time."

"All right. Do you think it's a good idea?"

"Why? Are you having reservations?" Chris watched as George tried to get past Gomez and Sanchez so she could get her parcel cart.

"I'm thinking of Jordan. Me popping back into her life and all."

Chris was astonished. This was thinking outside the box for B. "I don't think it's a bad idea if you have no intentions of getting back with Diane."

"I don't."

"Then you need to explain to Jordan that you're a friend, that you'll be there for her, but you're not a parent."

"I don't think she ever thought I was one. I'm more the play-date type," B. said.

"Then it's fine."

"Great. Thanks, Chris. I hope everything works out on your end too."

Chris clicked off. In the interim, Gomez and Sanchez had resolved their differences and were making plans to go to lunch.

"How about Twisters?" Gomez said.

"How about Pancho's and I'll buy," Sanchez replied.

"Deal."

"Chris, you want to go to Pancho's?" Sanchez asked.

"Uh, no, thanks. Last time I ate there I had the shits for a week."

"White girl," Gomez said, shaking his head.

"I know, but she always saves our ass. Go buy her a Coke," Sanchez said.

"Good idea."

They walked off together, leaving her to ponder how she came to be the babysitter of her friends and coworkers when she didn't parent herself nearly as well.

Her phone rang again. "Yes, B."

"Don't forget about tomorrow. The center people want us there two hours early to get set up."

"Great. See you soon," Chris said. She groaned. Tomorrow was the Fourth of July gay picnic. The only bright light was spending the day with Luce. Chris went back to her case and resumed putting her mail together. She picked up Veda Hidalgo's vacation hold and put in a slip to remind her. *Who in their right mind comes back from vacation the day before a holiday?* But then, Veda always did things a little differently.

George leaned over into Chris's case. "Is it always like this?"

"No, just Mondays, Wednesdays and Fridays."

"Something to look forward to," George said.

"It's just another day in the life of a mailman—or, if you prefer, letter carrier. Are you still going to the picnic tomorrow with—Rose?"

"Yes," she said, blushing slightly.

"Good."

The next day Chris, Luce, Amadeus and Midge stood at attention while they received instructions from Bev Samuels, the coordinator of the Albuquerque Gay and Lesbian Community Center. She was in charge of the "Second Annual Fourth of July Barbeque Extravaganza." Chris thought the extravaganza part was over the top, but who was she to argue with the semantics of community pride? Her attention wandered as a pack of giggling and squealing drag queens walked by in various stages of dress. Luce poked her in the ribs as Bev noticed she'd lost an audience member. From what Chris could gather, she was only to serve beer to people wearing pink wristbands. B. and Jude were in charge of selling tickets and issuing the pink bands after checking the person's identification. It didn't seem too difficult but Bev kept yapping on about it.

"Now, Chris, what's the first thing we check before we even start to pour an adult beverage?" Bev asked.

Bev had the uncanny ability to morph into a second-grade teacher. She had short brown hair with highlights, and several

125

areas of her body were pierced. Chris didn't want to imagine the other areas. She had wide hips and a butt to go with. Her turned-up nose was cute but the full mouth covered in red lipstick was another matter. Like someone told her if she wore lipstick she could pass if need be. She reminded Chris of the Joker in the Batman cartoons.

"Excuse me?" Chris asked.

"The beer," Luce prodded.

"A pink bracelet."

"Excellent. You two will do just fine. Now fly, little birds, off with the boys." Bev pointed in the direction of the beer tent.

"Like we don't fucking know where it is," Chris muttered. Luce pinched her. "Ouch."

"Deserved."

Bev said, "Now, Amadeus and Midge, you little darling, let's go to concessions and get things rolling."

Luce and Chris made their way to the beer tent where two burly guys in tank tops and tight cutoffs were unloading kegs of beer off a rented Budget truck.

"I know she's a little bossy, but that's why she's in charge," Luce said.

"I will not be placated by lame excuses for over-the-top Martha Stewartism."

Luce laughed. "Have it your way. Just be glad we're not in concessions."

"I fall down on my knees in gratitude for that one."

The burly guys looked up as they approached.

"Hi there, we're the beer girls," Chris said.

"Oh, my God, you survived the orientation. You poor things," the buff blond guy said.

"Barely. I had visions of Catholic school and Girl Scouts all rolled up in a rule-ridden nightmare," Chris replied.

The tanned guy with the shaved head burst out laughing. "This is going to be fun. I'm Dave and this is Stephen."

They shook hands. "I'm Chris and this is Luce."

"Are you together?" Stephen asked.

"Only in my dreams," Chris said.

Luce smiled sweetly.

"Oh, my God, get the camera. Single lesbians. It's a proverbial no-no. A moment in time when all has gone awry," Dave said, placing his hand on his heart.

"I certainly hope you do a little acting on the side," Chris said.

"Local theater and a comedy routine at the bar," Dave replied.

Luce eyed the pallet of melting ice. Stephen caught her gaze and said, "Uh, yeah, we better get that in those barrels before there's nothing left. Bev would have our balls." Both of them cupped their hands over their crotches. "No, Bev, don't do it. We promise to be good."

"You guys are too much," Luce said.

"That's why we can't get dates," Dave said.

"It's not like the old Harvey Fierstein days where a flamboyant, overwrought fag was appreciated," Stephen said.

"Oh, no, she's looking at us." Dave picked up a bag of dripping ice. "Evil, bossy lesbian."

"I hope you don't think we're all like that," Luce said, looking concerned.

"Of course not. Besides, if it wasn't for her take-charge attitude we'd still be in committee and there wouldn't be a picnic." He swung the bag of ice into the barrel and dripped water everywhere.

Chris surveyed the mass of people milling around and engaging in preparatory activities—putting up tents to sell trinkets, the sound guys setting up the stage, the drag queens trying out their moves. She could see B. and Jude getting the tickets and cashbox ready. B. and Bev had clashed earlier over whether B. could hand out her realty packets with the tickets. It smoothed over when B.

offered to cut Bev's sister a deal for selling her house. B. was resourceful. She'd taught the Pipster, who was dressed in a rainbow T-shirt, how to distribute tickets by pressing the red dispenser button on the cue of "Go." B. would get lots of calls for her services just from showing off the Pipster.

Chris helped Luce put the ice in large plastic barrels and then fill them with soda for the non-beer drinkers and the kids. They arranged the cups and put down plastic tablecloths over the laminated fold-up tables. These would be sticky and gross in a matter of minutes, Chris thought. "We need bar towels. Looks like little Miss Perfect forgot something."

Just then Bev came over with a box of cocktail napkins and several bar towels. "I forgot to give these to you at orientation. My mistake."

"Not a word," Chris said to Luce, who smiled smugly.

"I just wanted to thank you two in advance for your help, and I hope you're successful in your quest," Bev said. She winked at them and then bustled off.

Dave and Stephen peeked around the truck.

"You can come out now. The evil, bossy lesbian is gone," Luce said.

"Who spilled the beans?" Chris asked.

Luce cocked her head in the direction of Amadeus, who was standing in the concession tent not looking happy. Apparently there was a disagreement over paper aprons.

"Can't we go see how it turns out?" Chris asked, emptying the last bag of ice into the barrel. "There's nothing more entertaining than a pissed-off German giving someone a piece of her mind."

"All right. Boys, we're going to take a break before showtime," Luce called out. Dave and Stephen were riding kegs of beer and doing a cowboy scene from *Brokeback Mountain*.

"It's no wonder they don't have boyfriends," Chris said.

Dave broke out of character. "Don't do anything I wouldn't do."

"I couldn't do anything you do," Chris said under her breath. "At least they're not boring."

By the time they got to the concession stand, Amadeus was at full speed, approaching take-off.

"We almost missed it," Chris whispered.

"I'm telling you I'm not wearing a giant paper towel," Amadeus said, holding up the paper apron with obvious distaste.

"And I'm telling you, we can't be responsible for your clothing if you don't wear it," Bev said, her hands on her expansive hips.

"You look cute," Chris whispered to Midge, who was wearing the silly apron and pop-up chef's hat.

"I just did it to shut her up, but it's not working."

Luce stepped in. "Amadeus, I have a cloth apron in my truck. It's clean. Perhaps you could wear that instead."

"You're not cooking without one." Bev leveled her final charge.

Amadeus gave Chris a dirty look.

"Hey, this whole thing wasn't my idea."

"How about it?" Luce said.

"All right, for the group I will do it."

"I'm sorry, Midge. I only have one. I use it for setting up at the art fairs so I won't get dirty," Luce said.

"I'm fine," Midge said as she arranged the cooking utensils.

"I'll be right back with your apron, Amadeus," Luce said.

"Good luck, girls," Chris said. "I should get back. The ice is probably melted enough to put the soda in."

"I still don't like this," Amadeus muttered.

Chris left the counseling to Midge and trotted off to the beer tent. The boys were filling up beer cups in anticipation of the thirsty crowd.

"Welcome back to the ranch," Dave said.

"We're not still playing in the movies?" Chris asked.

"No, we're done with that," Stephen said.

"We've moved on to Name that Fruit," Dave replied.

"I don't even want to know," Chris said. She started dumping the soda into the barrel when a young woman dressed in a black security outfit came over.

"Mind if I snag one of those," she asked.

"No, go ahead. They're not real cold, though."

"I'm looking for the caffeine buzz," she replied, taking a Mountain Dew. "I worked the night shift at APD."

"I thought you looked familiar," Chris said, moving on to the next barrel, thinking she should have them filled by the time Luce got back.

"Did I arrest you once?"

"No, you arrested my friend's girlfriend for beating up her car."

"The BMW and the rolling pin."

"Yes. Amadeus is still leery of dating because she just got the insurance settlement and bought a Mercedes."

"Is she here?" the woman asked.

"She's doing food," Chris replied.

They were lighting up the large gas grills. Bev was having trouble with the grill lighter. Chris smirked. She delighted in watching control freaks have bad moments. It was like karma. This delight faded when she noticed that Midge's paper apron was on fire. Bev, it seemed, had been attempting to light the grill and Midge got caught in her crosshairs.

"Oh, shit," Chris said.

"What?" the police officer asked.

"Look!" Chris pointed to Midge.

"Come on," the woman instructed as they ran for the concession stand.

"Midge, you're on fire," Chris screamed.

Amadeus saw it first. "Oh, crap." She looked around for something to put her out with. She saw the barrels of ice that Chris had filled. Amadeus grabbed Midge under her arms and ran toward Chris and the police officer. Chris caught her gist and did an about-face. "Chris, get the pop out so we can put Midge in."

Chris and the officer frantically pulled the cans out and when Amadeus reached them, with Midge still in shock the barrel was mostly ice and water. Amadeus dumped her in. The fire fizzled out.

"Midge, are you all right?" Chris asked.

"If I had testicles they'd be up around my earlobes," Midge said.

Stephen and Dave stood staring. Bev came running with Luce in tow.

"Midge, my God! Amadeus was right—paper aprons are dangerous," Bev said, wringing her hands.

"Gee, Bev, since when are we grilling people?" Dave said.

"Look, it's a midget shish kebab," Stephen said.

Bev shot them a dirty look. She touched Midge's face. "You poor thing, you could have been killed."

"I think we need to get her out of there," Luce said. "She's turning blue."

"Please," Midge said.

Amadeus lifted her out. Bev dabbed her down with the bar towels.

"That was quick thinking," the police officer told Amadeus.

"Don't I know you?" Amadeus asked as she tied the apron on that Luce had given her.

"The rolling-pin incident. I was the filing officer."

"Oh, yes. Most unfortunate," Amadeus replied.

"I'm Elaine."

"It's nice to meet you," Amadeus said, extending her hand.

"Really, Bev, I'll just go home and change," Midge said, swatting away another one of Bev's bar towel rubdowns. "And how about I pick up a fire extinguisher in case we have another mishap."

"I'll drive you, and we'll stop for one. It's the least I can do. I wouldn't want you to mess up your car. Mine's a wreck anyway," Bev said.

Chris was imagining an Impala or an old Cadillac with the faux soft-top peeling off when Midge tugged at her leg. "If I'm not back in twenty minutes, call my cell," she said in a low voice.

"What's up?" Chris squatted down so they were eye-to-eye. They were standing in a pool of water.

"She scares me."

"Why? Does she like you?" Chris looked over at Bev, who was relaying information to her second in command. She was definitely ogling Midge.

Midge nodded.

"I thought that's what we're here for."

"Well, yes, but you see . . ." She would have continued but Bev grabbed her arm and was whisking her off. "Don't forget, Chris."

"I've got your back," Chris murmured to Midge. She watched as Bev trundled off with Midge, who looked terrified. Chris thought maybe it was Midge's fear that she would be swallowed up in Bev's enormous thighs.

"What's that about?" Luce asked, putting the soda back in the barrel.

"Bev's got the hots for Midge and she's afraid."

Luce laughed. "No way."

"I think it might be a size issue," Chris said as she set the alarm on her cell phone for twenty minutes.

"Are you going to save her?"

"If I have to."

The admission gates were open and the beer tent was the first place everyone went.

"I guess it's showtime," Chris said, trying not to get panicky as the thirsty hoard descended.

Twenty minutes had passed. Rose and George stopped by. Chris left them talking to Luce while she snuck behind the rental truck to call Midge, who sounded completely flustered.

"Are you all right?" When there was no response, Chris said, "Just answer yes or no."

"No."

"Do you want to get away from her?"

"Yes."

"Tell her things are really getting hectic here and we need her help immediately. She'll have you back here ASAP."

"I'll do that. Well, just try and hold down the fort until Bev gets there," Midge said, raising her voice.

"Good job."

"I owe you."

Chris chuckled. "See you soon." She clicked off and went back to help pour beer. She looked up to find Lola, the fly-ball coach, waiting for her.

"B. said I'd find you here."

Chris handed her a beer. Lola was dressed in close-fitting workout shorts and a black tank top. She looked fabulous. Chris mentally slapped herself like a fat kid in a candy shop about to break her diet. "Yep, just playing barmaid for the day."

Lola sipped her beer. "How have you been? I haven't seen you at practice lately."

"Oh, I've been working a lot of overtime. We get real short during the summer, vacations and all. The mail has to go through." Chris tried to seem nonchalant. She saw Luce watching them. She didn't want to fail this test. Lola's only potential was as a fuckmate. She was supposed to be looking for a partner inside as well as outside the bedroom. "B. says you've been teaching the Pipster a lot of new moves."

"That dog is simply amazing."

Chris noticed the beer line had dwindled. This was not good. It meant she could talk. "She sure is," she said, wiping the counter again.

"Chris, I wondered if maybe we could—"

She was interrupted by Luce, who grabbed Chris around the waist and kissed her cheek. "Come on. Stephen said he'd watch

133

the stand while we get something to eat." Then, seeming to notice Lola, she said, "Oh, hi, Lola."

Chris noticed the confusion in Lola's face. This was better than trying to explain what was really going on. "Well, let's go. I'm starving and I want to see if Midge has returned from the land of Bev."

"I just saw her in the restroom trying to get lipstick off. She's covered in it."

"Oh, no. She was attacked," Chris said, taking Luce's hand.

"We'll catch up with you later, Lola. Have fun," Luce said.

"Sure," Lola replied.

When they were out of earshot, Chris said, "Thanks for saving me." She dropped Luce's hand. Luce picked it back up. Chris pretended not to notice.

"It was my pleasure. Let's go find Midge."

They found Midge in the restroom scrubbing lipstick off her collar. She appeared to have removed the rest off her skin. Chris could still make out the blotches on her arms and legs where she'd been scrubbing. Her white polo shirt was not so fortunate, and her hair was messed up. She looked ravaged.

In the dimness of the restroom she peered at Chris and Luce with the look of an animal who had narrowly escaped the hunter.

"Midge, are you all right?" Luce asked.

"I'm fine. Goodness, that woman moves fast."

"Do you like her?" Chris checked for feet under the stalls. They were alone.

"Well, I'm not sure. She's a little aggressive for my taste."

Luce laughed and gave Midge a quick hug. "We'll find you the right one."

Midge smiled. "I might disappear into her hips and never return."

"Did I ever tell you about that dream I had?"

"The one about falling into the vagina?"

"You told," Chris said, pointing a finger at Luce.

134

Luce started to laugh. "I couldn't help myself."

They would have all rolled around on the floor had it not been the restroom. They composed themselves and went to find Amadeus. She was talking to Elaine, the police officer, who was doing security while Amadeus flipped burgers.

Everything was working out in a way, Chris thought as they joined B. and Jude along with the Pipster at one of the picnic tables. Amadeus was at least talking to a woman. B. had Jude. Midge had been tucked in tight with a woman she may or may not like, and she was hanging out with Luce. Perhaps this plan, this concerted attempt at love, did have merit.

Chris bit into her burger and smiled. Luce reached across the table and wiped her chin.

"Mustard?"

Luce nodded. "Are you happy?"

"I am, actually."

"Me too. Did you want that pickle?"

Chris handed it to her, thinking, *I would give anything you asked for including my heart.*

Chapter Fourteen

Later that night, Chris and Luce stood on the veranda of her house hugging their good-byes. This was a very long good-bye. B. had gone to Jude's condo for a nightcap. With a wink and a nod, Chris took this to mean she wouldn't be home until tomorrow morning around ten. The Pipster now had a bed of her own at Jude's. Chris knew this because B. would call her at work around ten to tell her she just got home and relay the rest of her day and the Pipster's. She couldn't decide if B. did this out of courtesy or if Chris had somehow become a human substitution for her Blackberry.

"Do you want to stay?" Chris asked.

"Are you working tomorrow?"

"No, it's my day off. Didn't that work out great? I swear that only happens, like, once every five years."

"Then I'd love to stay," Luce said.

"We can have a brandy. B. stocked the liquor cabinet with the good stuff."

"And how about a little music on the record player and a slow dance?"

"Wow, this'll be festive," Chris said, unlocking the door. Her heart rate increased and her nether regions did a loop-de-loop. The entire day at the barbeque had been a bagful of mixed signals. She reminded herself that Luce was off-limits.

Luce dug through the pile until she found the Ella Fitzgerald album *Someone to Watch over You.* "You might consider organizing these one day."

"B. will when she discovers them. I'm going to miss her compulsive organizing when she moves out."

Luce blew the dust off the turntable. "I can't believe you still have this thing. I love it. CD players don't have the same ambience as this." She carefully put the needle down on the record.

Chris poured the brandy. B. had bought proper glassware because she thought it lowbrow to pour good brandy into the jam jars that Chris used for orange juice. She handed Luce her glass. "I miss the old days of records. Don't get me wrong. My portable CD player has its merits but the cracks and hisses—" She shrugged. "The fidelity has so much more character."

"Are you nervous?" Luce asked. She sipped her brandy and stared at her.

"Me, nervous? Why?"

"Because you get wordy when you're nervous." Luce took her in her arms and made their bodies sway to the music. "Well, are you?" She slid her hands down Chris's back and onto her hips.

"Nervous, yes."

"About this?"

Chris pulled back and stared intently at Luce. She didn't know what to say or do. Fear clanked around in the back of her mind like a soda can bouncing and scraping across the pavement as the wind propelled it. The five seconds they stood there looking at each other spun into an eternity.

Luce took Chris's face in her hands and kissed her forehead, her now closed eyelids and then her mouth. Chris had often wondered what kissing Luce would feel like. Luce parted her lips. Their tongues danced around each other. Her heart pounded and then she experienced the vertigo of instantaneous sanity. She pulled away and blurted the worst possible thing. "I'm not Claire."

Luce smiled and the light caught her eyes. "I don't want you to be Claire."

"Then what's going on?" Chris tried to keep panic from making her the pebble in the slingshot of lost moments.

"My God, woman. You're going to make me draw this out," Luce said, pushing Chris's shoulders so she took a step back.

"I'm thickheaded."

"No, you're avoiding the obvious." She pushed her again.

"And what would that be?" Chris's mouth was dry and her tongue felt like sandpaper.

"I love you. You are the one I was meant to find when we started our journey into Date Night Club."

"Oh." Chris took another step back. They were in the hallway outside her bedroom.

"That's all you have to say?"

"All right. I've loved you from the moment I laid eyes on you. I wished you were mine and I've been drowning myself in nymphomaniacs trying to get over you, and now that we're here I'm scared shitless."

Luce laughed. "That's much better." She nudged Chris into the bedroom.

Standing at the foot of the bed, Chris asked, "Don't you think we should date first?"

"Chris!"

"I mean, this is a little sudden. Shouldn't we have a few dinners, go to a movie, buy flowers . . ."

Luce took off her shirt and slipped off her shorts.

"Oh, my," Chris said.

Luce pushed her down on the bed, straddled her and pulled off her shirt. The sports bra, however, proved to be a challenge. Chris, in an effort to be helpful, tugged at it as well, only getting it further stuck. They both laughed.

"What are these things? A lesbian chastity belt?" Luce said.

"Wait until you get to my underwear."

With a final tug, the bra broke free. Luce waved it around like a lasso.

Chris touched Luce's smooth, flat stomach. She wasn't scared anymore. Luce kissed her and undid her shorts, slipping them off. She ran her fingers under the waistband of Chris's panties, watching her face. When Chris let out a little moan, she pulled them off. She ran her hand between Chris's legs. Chris rocked her hips forward. Luce slipped her fingers inside, then she leaned down on her, kissing her, making love with her tongue and her fingers. Chris opened her legs wider. Before she knew it, her legs were wrapped around Luce's waist. Luce moved her hips in time with her fingers, pushing them farther inside. Chris moved against her hard and fast until they were rocking in unison. Chris came, not in her usual slow, languid, slip-in-the-backdoor style, but with a pounding burst of pure power. She felt like a rubber band sailing off into the wild blue yonder.

With her hand on Luce's lower back, she felt her tremble and her breathing grow ragged. "You didn't!"

"I couldn't help it," Luce said. She didn't look the least bit apologetic.

Chris rolled Luce on her back. "You better have another one in you."

"I'm sure we'll manage," Luce said, closing her eyes as Chris's tongue circled her nipple. "Chris?"

"Hmm," Chris said, looking up.

"I love you, you know that." Luce was serious.

"I certainly hope so. My sleeping-around days are over."

Chris kissed her stomach. She nibbled at the flap of skin that hovered like an eyelid over Luce's navel. For years she'd looked at it whenever Luce wore a short shirt or a tied- up one.

She went lower, guiding Luce's legs around her shoulders. She slipped her tongue between the pink folds and thrust it inside. Luce quivered. Chris inserted her fingers. She moved up so she could kiss Luce and feel her at the same time. "Is this all right?" She studied Luce's face.

"It's fabulous."

They moved together, slowly at first and then quicker until Luce cried out. Afterward, they lay in each other's arms, Chris nestled between Luce's firm, round breasts. She ran her fingertip around Luce's apricot-colored nipple. Chris gazed up at her. Luce was clearly happy.

Suddenly, Chris panicked. "What are we going to tell our friends?"

Luce pulled her back down. "Do you always worry this much?"

"Only when it's serious."

Luce kissed her. "We'll figure something out."

Chris rolled onto her back. "We're going to have to hide it." She leaned up on one elbow. "Not because I want to." She traced Luce's lips with her finger.

"Then why?"

"Because I want them to find girlfriends. If we're done, I know Amadeus and Midge will bail out. That's not right. The club credo will fall to dust and ruin."

Luce kissed her again. She pushed her back down and caressed her breast. "If it'll make you happy I'll be your secret mistress for as long at it takes." Her fingers caressed Chris's stomach.

Chris shivered. "That'll be great." She was aroused again. She guided Luce's fingers inside her.

"More?" Luce said.

"Oh, yes."

The next morning Luce and Chris were in the bath when Chris's cell phone rang. She had set it on the counter in case B. called. She didn't want any surprises—such as B. finding them in a compromising position that even B. could figure out despite living in a cloud of love and money.

"Where are you?" B. asked.

Chris thought about this for a moment. "I'm at the union hall."

"I thought you had the day off."

"I do. I had some unfinished business I needed to take care of." She tried not to moan as Luce took her nipple in her mouth.

"I'm making tamales tonight. Jude's going to help. I wanted to know if you and Luce were free. I've been trying to get ahold of Luce but she's gone missing. I wanted to use our kitchen because Jude's is too small."

"That sounds great. I'll run by Luce's when I'm done. She's probably working on some huge project and isn't answering her phone. Are you coming home to change?"

"I'm on my way now."

"Where are you?" Chris asked, trying not to voice her panic.

"I'm about to get off on the Carlyle exit. Why do you ask?"

"No reason. How's the Pipster?"

"Tired. She's going right to bed when we get home. She's taking the day off. No, I insist."

Chris heard the dog whining.

"Pippy, I'm telling you, you have to rest. You've got a game on Friday."

"B., if I could interrupt—"

"Hold on, Chris. Pippy is giving me some lip."

There was barking.

"B., I've got to go."

"All right, I'll see you later then."

Chris yanked Luce out of the bath. "We've got ten minutes."

They grabbed their clothes and flew out of the house. They turned the corner toward Central Avenue just as B. and Pippy pulled up in the drive. Chris hoped B. didn't notice the bath. She'd dried out the tub with towels and snatched up the bath mat, shoving everything in the washer. She leaned back in the seat. "That was close."

"I think my place is a much better idea," Luce replied. She squeezed Chris's hand.

"For the rest of the day?"

Luce smiled. "Oh, no." She looked over at Chris. "I don't have any socks."

"Do you want to go buy some?"

"No, you don't understand. I left them in the bathroom."

Luce had made love with her socks on because her feet were cold. It was one of their first intimate things.

"Chris?"

"What?"

"They're special socks."

"Because you wore them when we made love?" Chris asked, still off in la-la land.

"They're batik socks. You can't put them in the washer. The dye will run."

"You have hand-wash-only socks?"

"Like I said, they're special socks."

Chris remembered them. They were purple with deep red veins. "Now, where did you leave them?"

"In the bathroom by the bath mat."

"The one I scooped up with all the white towels." Chris got it. "Maybe B. won't run the washer."

"I'll buy you new towels."

"Luckily all B. washes is her underwear. Everything else is dry clean only."

"Sorry," Luce said. She looked pitiful.

"What's wrong with purple towels. I think those ones were heisted from the gym anyway."

They got on the freeway and headed toward Placitas.

"What are we going to do all day?" Chris asked.

"Eat, sleep, make love, repeat."

"Fantastic."

Later that evening when Chris and Luce reappeared at the house, B. was in the kitchen cooking. The first thing she said was, "Chris, have you seen my underwear?"

Chris faked a cough so she wouldn't laugh. "No. Have they gone missing?"

"No, they're purple." B. went to the laundry room and returned with a stack of neatly folded underwear.

Luce busied herself looking at the enchilada sauce cooking on the stove. She lifted the lid. "B., this smells great."

"Yeah, those are definitely purple. Is this something new for you?" Chris asked.

"They're supposed to be white. I put them in a load with the white towels that were already in the washer and they came out purple."

"Maybe we have a magic washer."

Luce stuck her head in the fridge but Chris could tell she was laughing.

"I think there's some Dos Equis on the bottom shelf."

"Then I found these weird socks." She held up Luce's batik socks. They seemed to have fared well.

"Huh, I must have left those in the washer last time I did a load. Sorry about your undies, B."

B. eyed her suspiciously. "These don't seem your style."

"I'm branching out."

Jude came in from B.'s room. "I think they look very sexy," she said, pointing to the stack of purple underwear.

B. smiled at her. "Did she finally go down?"

"Yes, eyes firmly shut, and she's snoring."

"Come see," B. said to Chris and Luce.

They tiptoed to the bedroom. The Pipster was sleeping, head on B.'s pillow, her lower half covered in designer sheets. She wore red pajamas with white bones on them.

"She's so tired. I had to take her to work. She insisted," B. whispered.

"I love her pajamas," Luce said.

"Aren't they darling? Jude found them in a catalog. Pippy just loves them."

Back in the kitchen, Jude asked Luce how batik worked. Chris figured that Jude had a pretty good idea about whose socks were in the washer. The arts fascinated Jude, who was endlessly quizzing Luce on how various things were created. Luce, on the other hand, had taken to asking Jude questions about the mechanics of structure. Jude was a civil engineer. Luce's art projects involved a lot of framing and hanging in site-specific areas. Jude was very good at coming up with solutions.

"You know, those socks look more like something Luce would wear," B. said. She took a hard look at Luce's outfit. She was wearing khaki shorts and a tie-dyed T-shirt.

Luce smiled.

As a distraction, Chris opened the oven and peered inside. The smell of corn and spicy beef permeated the kitchen. "B., these look great."

B. puffed up and left off the socks.

Jude hooked her arm around B.'s waist and kissed her cheek. "She's an amazing cook."

B. stood there beaming.

Chapter Fifteen

"How attached are you to that motorcycle?" Luce asked as she kissed the tan line running across Chris's lower back.

They'd made love all afternoon. Chris was supposed to be doing laundry and cleaning the house. That's what she told B. she was doing. B. seemed to have a new interest in Chris's schedule after the Fourth of July picnic and the socks incident. It was a week later and Chris's next scheduled day off. The week had been long as she and Luce had snuck around trying to get time alone.

Chris took her laundry to the cleaners, who charged by the pound, and called the Merry Maids to come clean the house. Luce was supposed to be working on a project for a juried show. She didn't know how Luce was going to make this time up. Maybe she could help her.

"I love my bike. Why?" Chris rolled over. She pulled Luce on top of her and ran her hands down Luce's sides, feeling her ribs and then positioning her hips so their wetness met. Luce let out a moan.

"I just wondered."

Chris cupped her hand around Luce's triangle of soft, curly hair. She slipped a finger inside. Luce moved against it. "More?" Luce nodded. She moved against her fingers. "Oh, yes."

The motorcycle discussion was benched. Chris knew what it meant. Now that Luce had given her heart, she didn't want to lose her in some terrible bike crash. Chris had been eyeing a Toyota Tacoma. It was for sale by a guy on her route. The price was reasonable. She knew the owner. He was meticulous. She planned to surprise Luce with her first sacrifice for love. True love was a weird thing. It made a lap dog out of the most hardened of skeptics. She'd sit up and roll over for Luce anytime.

When Luce cried out, Chris smiled. "I love you." She held Luce in her arms. She felt a rush of emotions—need, desire, tenderness and ultimately fear. She attempted to use the good feelings to snuff out the bad. But fear had kept her out of relationships. She would be forced to discover a new way to extinguish its reign.

Luce looked up at her and Chris glimpsed the solution—time. It would take time to nurture her abused heart.

She looked over at the clock. It was four thirty. "Oh, shit. I've got to go. B. will be home in an hour and I haven't picked up my laundry."

"I don't know how much longer I can do this."

Chris's heart skipped a beat. "Do what?" Alarmed, she grabbed her clothes and rapidly dressed. Was her heart to be abused already?

"Hide out. We haven't spent the night together since we became lovers. I want to wake up with you. I want to spend the weekend."

"Oh, that. Wow, you had me going for a minute." She sat on the edge of the bed and put her socks on.

146

The sheet barely covered Luce's bare shoulder. The sight made Chris weak. She wanted to stay.

"What were you thinking?"

Chris avoided her gaze. "Oh, nothing." She concentrated on tying her shoes.

"You thought I was dumping you."

"Maybe," Chris said.

Luce pulled her down, looking firmly at her. "I love you. That's not going to change. I'm not in this for a few hours spent in bed—lovely as they are. I want there to be an *us*. And at some point an *us* that lives together. Is that understood?"

"Yes, ma'am."

"All right. Now go before B. figures out what you're up to."

Chris got home ten minutes ahead of B. and the Pipster. She was putting her neatly folded clothes away. The house sparkled. It was well worth sixty bucks, she thought.

"The house looks great," B. said. She ran a finger along the top of the television. "You even dusted."

"How scary is that," Chris said.

B. smiled but continued her inspection. Chris followed her, hoping no clues had been left behind. She felt like an errant teenager who'd had a party and got the house in order before Mom and Dad got home. B. seemed suspicious.

"What?" Chris asked.

"You're never this thorough. Look at those faucets." They were standing in the bathroom. "They shine like brand new."

"I've found some better cleaning products."

"You must have. You've done wonders. I don't even clean this well, and I clean well."

The Pipster saved the day. She came in from the backyard.

"Did you go?" B. asked.

The Pipster barked.

"Number one or number two?"

147

The dog barked twice.

"Good girl." B. flipped out a black notebook from her breast pocket, looked at her watch and jotted down the information.

"What are you doing?" Chris asked.

"I'm charting her BMs." B. led them out of the bathroom and to the kitchen.

"What's that?"

"Bowel movements."

"Why?" Chris pulled two rib eye steaks from the fridge. They had decided that morning that they'd do steak, potatoes and salad for dinner. B. was a planner. This included the day's meals.

"To monitor her well-being and to keep track of her nutritional needs. Lola has all the dogs on a raw meat diet." B. pulled a long tube of the stuff out of the fridge and showed her. "You just squeeze it out into her bowl and it's much better than dry food, which is full of fat."

"I had no idea."

"Most people don't. I think it's greatly enhanced her performance. The championships are coming up and Pippy needs to be at her best. Don't you, baby." B. squatted down and stroked the dog's head. Pippy got up on her hind legs and put her paws on B.'s shoulders.

It was like she was hugging her. Chris was impressed. That dog had miraculously turned B. into a proper human being. She had become a caring, loving and compassionate person interested in something other than real estate and material wealth. She'd have to tell Luce.

"Oh, that's so sweet," B. said. "But it's power-nap time. Thirty minutes. I'll set my watch. Now off you go."

Pippy went to the living room and climbed up on the couch. She dutifully closed her eyes.

"Good girl."

"Doesn't she nap at the office?" Chris pictured the pristine real-estate office.

"Heavens, no. She works. She's in charge of meet-and-greet. That dog is worth her weight in gold. Clients come in all stressed out and nervous. Pippy puts them at ease."

"Have you met anyone who doesn't like dogs?" Chris pulled out the tomatoes and the mixed greens.

"Not many. If they don't I send them down the hall. We aren't going to connect. I don't waste my time."

Down the hall in B.'s world meant the lesser Realtors—the low producers. B. was the queen of the office and as such she decided which clients were worthwhile.

Chris watched as B. neatly wrapped the potatoes in tin foil. She was going to miss these times once B. decided to move on. But then she would probably move in with Luce. Her time of living alone had come to an end.

"After the championship I think we should sell the house."

"Excuse me?"

"Look, you're going to move in with Luce. I suggest you plan to do it over Labor Day weekend. A long weekend is always a plus when relocating."

Chris felt like one of B.'s clients.

"I'm already looking for a house for Jude and me and . . ."

Chris filled in the blank. "And the Pipster."

"Really?" B. said. She gave Chris a bone-crushing hug.

"What, you'd stay with me because of the Pipster?"

B. was resolute. Chris could tell. "Yes. I never felt like this about anyone else."

"Are we talking about Jude or Pippy?" She already knew the answer. Jude might last but Pippy was there for the long haul.

"Both." B. avoided Chris's gaze and dumped the bag of mixed greens into a teak salad bowl.

"Equally?" Chris asked.

"Of course," B. said as she searched the drawer for the salad tongs.

"I don't believe you."

B. rolled her eyes. "All right, I will always love Pippy more than any woman, excepting you. You're avoiding the entire issue. You and Luce aren't being honest with anyone."

"I don't know what you're talking about."

"Now, why would I say that you and Luce are going to live together?" B. put her hands on her hips, which meant she wasn't giving up until the truth came out. This was her all-business stance and Chris knew she was doomed.

"To save on expenses."

"Lame. If you think I don't know what's going on between you two, you're in complete denial. I see it written on your face everytime you come home."

"See what?" Chris made a last-ditch effort to save the secret. She knew it was useless.

"Chris."

"All right. We're madly in love."

"Why are you keeping it a secret?"

"Because we wanted everyone to find a partner first. If it looks like we're out of the running, then Amadeus and Midge will quit looking."

"I found someone, and that didn't stop anything."

"B., think about it. One person doesn't alter the group dynamics that much. But three out of five does."

B.'s face resembled a novice instantaneously experiencing a revelation. "Oh, I get it. That's so sweet."

"Sweet but difficult. If you can see it, do you think the others have?"

"Definitely not. I ran it past Jude and she thought I was nuts."

"And Jude is a lot like Amadeus in the introspective, intuitive department. Midge might have caught on by now. She's quick."

"Which I find refreshing. I've discovered that women are much harder to deal with because of their high degree of sensitivity." B. chopped the tomatoes with force.

Chris laughed. "That's putting it politely."

"Does that mean I admire Jude's butch behavior?"

"Yes."

"Diane used to get angry with me because I couldn't read her moods or understand that when she said nothing was wrong, something was wrong."

"That no really meant yes." Chris got out a cruet and dumped in a packet of Italian dressing mix. She pulled the oil and vinegar from the cupboard.

B. looked relieved. "Then it's not just me."

Chris smiled at her. B. was growing up to be a proper lesbian—finally. "Women are complex creatures. Why do think men have such a hard time?"

"But we should do better. As women, we should understand the female phenomena."

"Some women are beyond comprehension. Does Jude always say what she means? Ask for what she wants in a direct way?"

"Why, yes." B. blushed.

Chris guessed this meant sexually as well. "That's because you two are better matched. She doesn't mind your type-A behavior because she understands it, even admires it."

"She does. She never gets bent out of shape if I'm running late because I'm trying to cinch the deal. She's very flexible."

"Jude, it seems, values independence."

"You seem different."

B. was right. The past week had made her lucid, as if she was experiencing reality for the first time. The world and her perception were clearer, more concise. "Me? Come on. Let's put those steaks on the grill."

"It must be Luce's good influence."

They went out back and Chris sparked the grill. She put the steaks and potatoes on. She cheated by microwaving the potatoes first; otherwise they took too long on the grill. Luce would have parboiled them. She was going to have to get used to living without a microwave as Luce thought them evil. She smiled. She'd get used to anything for Luce. "What? I'm not good on my own."

B. raised an eyebrow.

"All right. I suck on my own."

"Better." B. flounced down on a chaise lounge. "I mean, you're less sardonic, more compassionate—almost sweet sometimes."

"Stop it, already. I'm going to puke. You want another beer?"

"Please."

She ran into Pippy coming out. She must have smelled the grilling meat. Chris patted her head. "Yes, you can have the bone." Pippy curled her black lips into what Chris was certain was a smile.

Chapter Sixteen

"You're going to love her," Ramon Ruiz told Chris as he tucked the cashier's check in his shirt pocket. He handed her the keys and the bill of sale. She'd gone to his house the next day to see if she could buy his silver Toyota Tacoma truck. It was in great shape and only had 56,000 miles on it. Chris knew Luce would be ecstatic. Ramon helped her load her motorcycle into the truck bed.

"Thanks, Ramon. I'll take good care of her."

"Great." He ran his hand along the edge of the truck bed. He was a large, dark-haired Hispanic who was about to become a father who needed a minivan.

Chris sensed he was torn between his life as an urban vaquero and a suburban father of small children in car seats. His life was changing as was hers. She'd have to sell the bike. Having it sit in the garage would be too much of a temptation.

"Her name is Twanda." Ramon's eyes grew moist. He twisted his mustache.

"Whose name?"

He cocked his head in the direction of the truck.

"Oh, sure. That's a great name. Isn't that from the movie *Fried Green Tomatoes?*"

"Yeah, loved that movie." He gave her a this-is-just-between-us glance.

"Me too." She didn't ask if a box of Kleenex had been present at his movie-going.

"What are you going to do with your bike? Are you going to keep it?"

"Nah. I bought the truck because the bike makes my girl-friend nervous. I'm going to have to get rid of it. I guess we all got to grow up sometime."

Ramon laughed. "Yep, love has a mighty high price tag."

"But they make us do it because they love us. So it's not such a bad trade-off." She looked mournfully at her motorcycle and Ramon did the same at his truck. "Buy some really cool wheels for the minivan and tint the windows. Dads can still be hip."

Ramon smiled. "Good idea. Keep your leather jacket."

"Take care." Chris got in the truck and made her way home.

Later that evening B. and Luce pulled up together. They'd gone for a massage and spa treatment at the Embassy Suites. One of B.'s clients had given her a gift certificate. Luce was the only one girly enough to go.

"It was fabulous," B. said as they came in the door.

Chris gave Luce a hug. "You smell wonderful."

"Sea salt, lemon grass and almond oil facial," Luce replied.

"Who's here?" B. asked as Pippy licked her face. The Pipster had had to remain home while B. was gone. She'd clearly suffered separation anxiety.

"No one," Chris replied.

B. pulled an Old Roy treat out of her pocket and handed it to the dog. "I love you too, Pippy. The dog took it gently and headed out back. "Where'd the silver truck come from?"

"It's mine. I bought it today from a guy on my route."

Luce and B. stared at her. "Why?" B. asked.

"Because I need side panels and an air bag." Chris avoided their gaze. "How about a beer?"

"You did it for me," Luce said, her face glowing. Chris wasn't sure if it was love or the aftereffects of the facial.

Luce took her face in her hands and kissed her. Chris melted, basking in the moment.

"Oh, crap!" Luce pulled away and looked in horror at B. "I forgot."

"She knows already," Chris said.

B. stood, hands on her hips. She was smiling. "And I figured it out all on my own."

"The conspiracy grows," Luce said.

"We're going to have to tell them."

"I don't see why this is such a big deal. The quest will go on because it's not finished. No one leaves the theater until . . ." B. appeared stumped.

"The fat lady sings," Chris finished for her.

"Precisely, or in our case, until the surly German and the short lady find lovers. I won't allow failure." B. looked resolute.

"All right. Let's tell them after the Pippy's fly ball championships," Luce said.

"Which we are going to win," B. said.

"B., your level of confidence never ceases to amaze me." Chris shook her head.

"Years of practice and a couple hundred self-improvement books, not to mention the seminars."

"Really?" Chris said.

"Yes. Do you think it's easy for a South Valley girl to completely repackage herself? Statistically speaking, I should be selling lottery tickets at the local convenience store, not upscale homes to the wealthy." B. straightened her linen blazer as if she were reminding herself how far she'd come.

"You're amazing," Luce said, giving B. a hug. "I think we all forget that sometimes."

"Thank you, Luce. That was very kind." B. moved to the kitchen window to check on Pippy.

"Now about those beers." Chris pulled three Coronas from the fridge and went out back with Luce and B.

The following day at work, Chris was stating union business during the weekly stand-up meeting. "One of our brethren has fallen on hard times. Alan Montoya has suffered a broken back and will be in traction for several months. He has no remaining sick leave so we're asking for annual leave donations."

Her request was met with a cacophony of catcalls.

Someone shouted, "Then he should have shown up for work more often."

"Why should I give that piece of shit anything?" someone else called out.

"What sort of man lets his wife run him over with his own damn car?" Garcia said.

Chris gave him a dirty look; that was supposed to be a secret. *The cat's out of the bag now*, she thought wryly.

"That's enough," said Harrison, the new supervisor trainee. Sid, the supervisor, nodded his approval.

"Look, I've got an offer. I'm raffling off my motorcycle. One ticket per eight hours of leave donation to Alan."

"What!?" Garcia said. "Chris, have you lost your mind?"

"It's my bike and Alan needs help." She could see the guys thinking about it. She'd gotten the go-ahead from the higher-ups. She could donate to a fellow employee. What Alan needed most was an allotment. She thought about selling her bike and giving him the money, but she knew he would never take it. This way it looked like his fellow employees had come to his aid.

A line formed and Chris gave out a ticket stub for each completed annual donation slip. Some guys with a lot of annual bought more than one.

"Now, my only stipulation is that Alan never knows about this. Understood?"

They all nodded. Chris put the slips in Garcia's ball cap. She had Sid pick a ticket. He pulled out the slip and read the name. "Ron Gomez."

Gomez jumped up and down. He gave Chris a bear hug and then picked her up and swung her around, yelling, "I won, I won, I won. I never win anything and today I won."

"You should have won—you donated a week of annual," Sanchez said.

Chris rolled her eyes. Those two would never stop bickering. They might as well be married.

"Yeah, and better than that, now I can't go to Marge's family reunion. Damn!"

"You can go riding with me now," Sanchez said, brightening at the idea.

"No shit," Gomez said. "Why'd you think I did it?"

They gave each other a manly nod.

"Here's the keys," Chris said, tossing them at Gomez.

"Let's go look at it," Sanchez said.

Gomez checked out Sid's reaction. "Go," Sid said.

"I've got an extra leather jacket," Sanchez said as they headed for the door.

"How much did you get?" Sid asked Chris.

She totaled up the number of slips. "Two hundred and forty hours."

"That'll get him through. He can come back on light duty." Sid took the annual donation slips from Chris.

"Now, all we have to do is keep him away from that lunatic wife," Chris said.

"It shouldn't be too hard. The judge gave her eighteen months."

"He could find a new girlfriend in that amount of time," George said.

Chris smiled at her. *Everyone in love thinks everyone can find love.* George and her girlfriend Rose were still going strong.

"I'm thinking," Sid said.

"How about a station picnic?" Garcia piped in as the stand-up ended and people were filtering back to their cases.

"And start up a coed softball league?" Kathy, the reworks clerk, added.

"I've missed that," Chris said. She used to play shortstop.

"And bowling, that's always a good time," Mary said.

They all laughed. "Boy, do we stick together or what. We don't even like the guy and look at us playing matchmaker to save his scrawny ass from that crazy ball-banging bitch." Mary was shaking her head.

They all laughed again.

"Mary! I can't believe you said that," Chris said.

"I just call it like I see it," she replied. Still shaking her head she went back to her case. She turned back around. "It was still nice what you did, Chris. The Lord Almighty gonna smile on your ass."

Later that evening, Chris was nestled in Luce's arms and running her fingers around Luce's nipple. They were spending the night at Luce's as Chris had taken annual for the following day. "I got rid of the bike today."

"Oh, I hadn't noticed."

Chris knew she was trying to be nonchalant. "I bet," she said, straddling her and caressing her sides.

Luce quivered. "Please don't." She was ticklish. This was news to Chris, who had inadvertently discovered it the other day. Chris moved in for the kill. "All right. I wondered if you were going to get rid of it. I was worried."

"That's better." Chris leaned down and kissed her.

"Yes, much better," Luce said as she pulled Chris up toward her. Her tongue traced the folds of Chris's nether regions.

"Oh, my."

The next morning Luce and Chris sat on the veranda drinking coffee. The gentle morning light danced off the plants still glistening from their morning watering.

"So we're going to do it this weekend?" Chris inquired.

"Do what?" Luce was perusing a garden catalog.

Chris leaned over to see she was studying the bulb section. She wanted to plant a bulb garden after admiring Chris's daylilies. They were great subject matter, according to Luce. She was going to enter one of her stained-glass works featuring bulbs into the juried show at the New Mexico State Fair in the fall.

"Tell Amadeus, Midge and Jude about us. You know, on the way to Pippy's fly ball championship game."

"Oh, yes. Now, why are we doing it then? I thought we were waiting until after the game. I mean, don't you think it might prove to be distracting?" She sipped her coffee and looked beautiful, so serene and sensual.

Chris could have ravished her right there except that Luce seemed so at peace. Sometimes she felt like a medieval friar straight out of Chaucer, lusting after pure-hearted women. She was going to have to learn to control herself. Luce was patiently waiting for her response. "I decided if we tell them on the way they will be distracted by the game and won't have time to fume. Amadeus is the only one I'm worried about."

"You're nervous about this."

"Is it that obvious?"

"Yes. It wasn't a nice thing to do, hiding it, but we did it out of love." Luce got up, kissed her forehead and went to refill their coffee cups.

Chris leaned back in her chair and watched the perfect white puffy clouds begin to obscure the blue sky. She hoped it wasn't a portent.

Chapter Seventeen

"Is everyone comfortable?" Amadeus asked.

They were stuffed into her Mercedes sedan, ready for the fly ball championships after gathering first at the Zoo for a quick breakfast.

"If you like being a sardine," Chris said.

"I'm telling you, this is a good idea. Parking will be at a premium. This is a big event," B. said.

"Easy for you to say," Chris muttered. B. was sitting in the front seat with Pippy on her lap. They were dressed in matching black Nike starter suits. If they hadn't looked so cute they would have looked stupid.

Amadeus started the car. Chris took Luce's hand, bracing herself. She had to jump now or she wouldn't do it. Midge, who was sitting next to Luce, looked down at their interlocked hands and raised her eyebrows. "Everyone, Luce and I have something to tell you."

Amadeus glanced at her rearview mirror.

"You see, we've gotten so close lately and our quest has only heightened this feeling—"

"What the hell are you talking about?" Amadeus said.

"Chris and I are lovers," Luce replied.

"We didn't tell you because we didn't want Date Night Club to end without finding everyone a beloved partner," Chris said.

"How long?" Amadeus asked, her steely eyes peering in the rearview mirror at Chris.

"About a month. Since the Fourth of July picnic."

"So we're charity cases, is that it?" Amadeus slammed the car in gear and hit the gas. Her car was parallel parked out in front of the restaurant. Unfortunately, she'd stuck the car in reverse and smacked into the car parked behind them. Everyone's head snapped back at the impact.

Chris was the first to turn around and look.

Amadeus had her eyes screwed shut. "What did I hit?"

"Just a police car." Chris gulped.

"Oh, shit!" Amadeus leaped out of the car.

The police officer was already surveying the damage. Chris rolled down the window and said, "It was all my fault."

Amadeus, seeming to suddenly remember the last few minutes, glared at her.

"And how would that be, since you're sitting in the backseat like a sardine?"

"I know it's horrible. No elbow room," Chris replied. "Hey, don't I know you? You're Elaine."

She smiled. "Rolling pin," she said, pointing at Amadeus. "Fire." She pointed at Midge.

"That's us," Chris said. "The queens of disaster."

"I still want to know how this is your fault."

"Well, you see we have this Date Night Club, which was designed to find us all proper girlfriends. B. found Jude at the book club, and Midge got jumped at the community picnic, although that didn't work out that well."

Midge nodded.

"And then, well, Luce and I got together."

"We didn't tell them until just now when Amadeus slammed into your car," Luce said.

"So you see, I'm the charity case. I got upset and put the car in reverse instead of drive." Amadeus stared at her shoes.

Chris thought this a humble gesture for the mighty amazon.

Elaine touched her shoulder. "There's no damage. The police cruisers have huge bumpers. We use them to push cars. And yours looks fine. Would you like to go to dinner with me tonight?"

Amadeus looked startled. "You want me to go to dinner with you?"

"Not as a charity case, if that's what you're thinking."

"I can't. I'm going to Pippy's championship game and then back here for the post-game festivities."

"Elaine could join us," Chris said. She refrained from saying "you bozo." "I mean, it is a restaurant." She did give Amadeus her you-stupid-fucking-moron look. She apparently got the point.

"Of course, that's a fabulous idea. Would you?"

"Sure. I'm off at six," Elaine said.

"See you then," Amadeus said, her face red.

When she got back in the car. B. punched her in the arm. "You need some lessons in how to get a date."

"Not anymore," Amadeus said. Pippy licked her cheek. Amadeus only grimaced slightly. She started the car and carefully pulled into traffic.

B. was correct about the parking. She didn't say anything but her vindication was evident as they slid into the last parking space in the lot. Everyone else would be looking for spots on the street. Chris was amazed at the crowd of people, dogs, referees and kids. Three months ago she had no idea this sport existed.

Pippy was barking and jumping around while B. got her sports bag out of the trunk. "I know, sweetie. Hold on. I'm excited too but you've got to conserve your energy."

Pippy sat down, her eyes never leaving B. *Pippy's speech coach must really be helping*, Chris thought. The dog's vocabulary and comprehension skills were better than a lot of her coworkers'.

Luce came up behind her. "What are you thinking about?"

"Just how smart Pippy is."

"She would've been toast if you hadn't come along," Amadeus said, pulling a cooler from the trunk.

B. glared at her.

"It's true," Amadeus shot back.

"I don't think now is the appropriate time to bring up Pippy's unfortunate turn of events. We are only concerned with the present, right, Pippy?"

Pippy barked. Midge squatted down and was rubbing lavender balm on Pippy's pads. She lifted each foot up as Midge instructed. Other dogs passed by but Pippy ignored them. Chris admired her single-mindedness. *Never let the competition psych you out.* Pippy had it down. She was the one that did the psyching.

"Where's Jude?" Luce asked as they made their way to the stands.

"She'll be here. She had something to do first." B. scanned the crowd for her.

"There she is," Midge said, pointing down onto the field.

Jude waved at them. She had set up a large gold and white banner that read, "Go Champs!" and on either side were two dozen red roses in vases sitting on small folding tables. Each table also contained a silver bucket with ice and Champagne and a bowlful of biscuits.

"Oh, my, how sweet is that," B. said, clutching her hands over her heart. Pippy looked up at her. "Pippy, look what Jude did for us."

Pippy must have noticed the biscuits because she pulled on the leash.

"You better go. We'll get seats." Chris leaned down and patted the dog's head. "I know you can do it, girl."

Pippy barked.

Amadeus knelt down and whispered something in Pippy's ear. The dog appeared to listen intently. Midge kissed her and Luce gave her a quick shoulder rub.

B. dabbed her eyes with a tissue. She'd gotten misty. "Thanks, guys. We couldn't have better friends, could we, Pippy?" She straightened her shoulders, took a deep breath and marched them both down to the field. Their regality was evident as they passed through the crowd.

The rest of them took their seats in the bleachers. It couldn't have been a more perfect day, Chris thought. The sky was clear and sapphire blue. The morning was still cool. She was acutely aware of this as she sat down on the cold metal bleachers. "Wow," she said, shifting uncomfortably.

Luce pulled out a fleece blanket from her knapsack. Chris helped her spread it out. Everyone sat back down and let out a collective sigh.

Chris smiled at Luce. "You must have been a Girl Scout."

Luce took her hand. "I like to be prepared."

Below them, B. and Pippy were wrapped up in pregame strategies. Lola appeared to be briefing them on what to do. Jude stood in the background. Her adoration for B. was apparent.

"They make a sweet couple," Luce said.

"Who? B. and Pippy?" Chris replied.

Luce pinched her thigh. "You know who."

Chris rubbed her thigh and tried to look pained. "They do. I'm so glad B. found furry love and human love. She's become a much better person for it."

"I think love makes us all better."

"It does," Midge agreed.

Chris studied her face and wondered if she'd gone off to that place where love was real and present. It was at this moment that Chris figured out what she would do to get Midge a partner. As

165

the four-dog teams lined up for the relay races, she worked out her plan. She would keep it a secret and make it the final crescendo of Date Night Club. In her mind's eye it was stunning. She hoped reality wouldn't ruin it.

Pippy's team easily won their first race. The Pipster always ran last of the four dogs because she was the fastest. Her time often gave them the added seconds the team needed to win. They watched as B. and Lola discussed strategy. Pippy stayed by B.'s side, looking up attentively. Chris wondered how much of the conversation the dog understood. B. had told her that dogs acutely desire to comprehend their human friends. The speech coach helped. What kind of world would it be if dogs could talk back? What would they say?

Luce leaned over. "What are you thinking about now?"

"If dogs could talk, what they'd say."

Luce laughed. "I know what Pippy'd be saying right now. She'd look over at the opposing team and say, 'I'm not afraid of you and I'm going to beat your ass.'"

Amadeus looked over, raising her eyebrow. "How long have you two been hanging out together?"

"What are you implying?" Luce asked.

"Things are changing," Amadeus replied.

"Oh, you mean my new sassy attitude. I'm kind of liking it," Luce said.

Midge smiled. "I think it suits you."

"Thank you, Midge," Luce said, taking Chris's hand.

"'Beat your ass' should be the team's mission statement," Chris said, glancing down at the dogs.

"That would go perfect with their name, the Blackhearts," Midge said.

"I don't get that name. Are the dogs depressed or something?" Amadeus asked.

They heard screaming from the field. B. was jumping up and down hugging Jude and Lola. The Blackhearts had made it to the semifinals.

166

Chris returned to the topic at hand. "No, Amadeus, it's the name of Joan Jett's band. She was this hard-rock lesbian who fronted the band and wrote the music. It's the perfect name for the team. It's like they're the bad boys and girls of fly ball."

"Lola is a great coach," Luce said.

Chris chuckled.

"What?" Luce asked.

"You were kind of jealous of her earlier."

Luce pursed her lips. "Well, maybe. I just didn't think she was in your best interest, that's all."

"She wasn't," Amadeus said. "So what do you guys think about Elaine?"

"She's got a career," Luce said.

"She's buff," Chris said.

"I think she really likes you. Didn't you two talk at the picnic?" Midge asked.

"Yes, but then there was the fire and after that she had to go break up a fight between two drag queens and we never got a chance to finish."

"So you lost your chance and then you sat on your stuck-up ass and did nothing about it. What happened to the womanizer I used to know?" Chris asked.

"Someone destroyed my car with a rolling pin," Amadeus replied.

"You're going to have to get over that," Luce said.

"She's right. Things will always happen in our lives that we'll trip over unless you choose to move it to the side so it no longer constricts your movements," Midge said.

"Wow, that's deep, Midge," Chris said.

"Years of therapy," Midge said. "Oh, speaking of that, I think we have an issue down on the field."

B. was wildly waving her arms and Jude was running toward the stands. "B. needs you guys down on the field," Jude said, leaning down to catch her breath. It was an impressive hundred-yard sprint.

That woman would walk over hot coals if B. asked her to, Chris thought.

"What's wrong?" Luce asked.

"B. called a time-out. This is the last race for the championship and they're behind. Pippy has to run faster than ever before. B. thinks we need group energy to stoke her up."

"All right, girls, it's time for action." Amadeus leaned over to the woman sitting next to her and said, "Could you watch our stuff for a minute? We have a championship to win."

They followed Jude back down to the field where B. was talking to Lola. B. glanced up. "I'm so glad you're here. Now gather 'round. Pippy, get in the middle and everyone focus positive energy on her."

Holding hands and closing their eyes, they encircled the dog. Chris wondered if this was some psyching-up thing B. had learned in one of her sales seminars. Her eyes sprang open when Pippy let out a primordial howl as if she were a Barbarian about to descend upon the Romans and take over the civilized world. Her teammates piped in and suddenly the field became a yowl fest. If this didn't scare the competition, Chris thought, nothing would.

Pippy lined up for her race. It was make or break. Chris prayed she'd win for B.'s sake or they'd never hear the end of it. She put her hands together and whispered, "Please, Pippy, I know you can do it."

Luce put her arm around Chris's shoulder. "I didn't know this meant so much to you."

"It doesn't, but B. will be insufferable if they don't win."

Luce laughed. She took off her crystal necklace and tied it around the dog's neck. "For good luck and great speed, Pippy."

The dog seemed to curl her lips up in a smile. The buzzer went off and Pippy hit the field.

Lola timed her run to the end of the course where she grabbed the ball and started her return. She looked over at B. "She needs three seconds on the return."

B. screamed, "Pippy, now, do it now!"

Chris wondered if B. had taught Pippy some new secret weapons technology. She wouldn't put it past her. Suddenly in the last four feet of the course, Pippy leaped up and crashed through the finish line. She had jumped the end of the course and beat her own record by five seconds. The other team owners looked on in astonished amazement.

B. and Lola were jumping up and down in jubilation.

"When did you teach her that?" Lola asked.

"I took her through an agility training course they had set up because I think she has potential and fly ball is almost over. She can jump. So I figured why couldn't we incorporate jumping into fly ball. It saves time," B. replied.

Pippy came over after she'd stopped by the biscuit stand and had a drink of water. B. swooped her up, kissing her and uttering things about how incredible she was. The dog was in heaven.

"I wish someone loved me that much," Chris said.

"You didn't just win the fly-ball championship. But I do love you a lot," Luce said.

Amadeus patted Pippy on the head and said, "Good job. I knew you had it in you. You are, after all, a German."

Midge snickered. "Boy, that doesn't show up much."

"What?" Chris asked.

"A compliment *and* national pride."

"Maybe she is ready for a girlfriend," Luce said.

The whole team went to the Zoo restaurant. The dogs were allowed inside because the sponsors had booked it as a private party. Amadeus and Rose had decorated the inside and made it dog-friendly. There were buckets full of balls, water bowls, biscuit bowls and little party hats. It was darling.

B. walked in first, leading Pippy, who was now dressed in a gold starter pullover with the word Champ embroidered on the back. She was still wearing Luce's crystal, her token of good luck.

"Look, Pippy, the dog world has gone from bakeries to a high-class restaurant."

"Don't get too used to it," Amadeus said.

"Hey, I hear there's big money in people wanting more pet-friendly establishments," Luce said.

"Really?" Amadeus said, appearing to take in her new clientele.

"You might think about having one night a week as a trial," Midge suggested.

The dogs were in heaven as they came in. They were to have roast beef sandwiches.

"This is just marvelous," Lola said.

Pippy sat by B.'s side while people and their pets were seated. Then they took a central table and B. banged a glass with a spoon. *Oh, no*, Chris thought, *not a speech*.

"I just wanted to thank all of the volunteers and our fabulous coach for the amazing season we've had. I can't believe how fast and how far we've come. To think of Pippy's humble beginnings and her rise to this place of honor is simply remarkable."

"I thought we weren't supposed to mention her upbringing," Amadeus whispered.

"Only during pregame, I guess," Chris said.

"I can't believe we won, and although winning isn't everything, it is awfully nice."

"Yeah, right," Amadeus muttered under her breath.

"I heard that," B. said. "Oh, look, your date is here." She pointed at Elaine, who'd just come in the door. The whole room stared.

Elaine waved cordially. She seemed to take it in stride. Amadeus was mortified. "I'm going kill her," she said, getting up.

"Not now. You'll ruin Pippy's moment," Luce whispered.

"As I was saying before I got rudely interrupted, I'm glad you're all here, and good job." B. finished by starting to applaud, and then the dogs howled. It was quite the noise but everyone looked happy.

Chapter Eighteen

"Holy shit!" Chris said as she checked her e-mail. It had been a month since the fly-ball tournament and the birth of her brilliant idea for Midge's love life. She didn't expect it to take off like this. Every day since she'd put out the call, her inbox was packed with requests for information.

"What are you up to?" Luce asked.

"Nothing really." Chris clicked to the home page so Luce couldn't check out her e-mail.

Luce sat on the corner of her desk and peered at her. They'd moved in together over Labor Day weekend to Luce's place and it was an adjustment. They'd taken one of the smaller unused bedrooms and turned it into an office for Chris. Both of them were used to living alone and now, as a couple, they kept tripping over each other. Chris didn't necessarily find this so hard because she'd done that with B. until they found their rhythm. It was

Luce she was worried about. She'd been alone for a long time and now there was always that other person trying to help or taking a shower when you needed the bathroom or watching a show when you liked another one.

"You're not one of those Internet porn people."

"No. I'm planning a surprise for a friend."

"Is it someone I know?" Luce asked.

"Very well."

"So you're researching things."

"Exactly. You know, we need to talk. B. is serious about buying the house but I'm concerned with our living arrangements." B. was still living with Pippy at Chris's house. She'd made a formal offer. It was all chop-chop with B. She wanted an answer now and she wanted it to be yes.

"What?" Luce looked alarmed.

"I mean, it's not easy living with someone, and I'd understand it if you wanted a lover but not a housemate."

"Is this about the dishwasher?" Luce asked, getting off the desk and moving to the couch. She took off her shoes and rubbed her feet. She'd been doing a big project for a bank downtown and putting in a lot of hours.

"The dishwasher?" Chris whirled around in her office chair. Luce looked lovely. Her hair was sort of half up and half down. She was wearing cut-offs and a tight white T-shirt.

"When I thought it was dirty and in fact you'd run it and then you put the dishes away because you thought they were clean and I'd mixed dirty ones in with the clean ones."

"Oh, that. Well, I suppose it's a manifestation of that. I just kind of feel like I'm intruding on your space. Like I'm in the wrong spot all the time. Maybe it's just paranoia."

"Come here," Luce said, patting the couch. Chris obeyed and Luce took her hand. "I love living with you. I'm stressed out about this deadline. I hate deadlines. If I've been less than ideal in paying attention to things, it has nothing to do with you."

"You're stressed." Chris couldn't believe it. Luce had always seemed so laid-back like the fucked-up things in the world didn't get to her.

"I can be stressed."

"Yes, you can be stressed. I just didn't know that you got stressed. Why didn't you tell me? I'm good at decompression." Chris leaned over and kissed her neck. She ran her hand up Luce's naked thigh. They were short cut-offs.

"Because I wanted everything to be perfect."

"You've got to lighten up." Chris kissed her ear.

"I'll try," Luce said, pulling off her T-shirt.

"There, that's better," Chris said, pushing her back onto the couch.

"Oh, much better," Luce said, unbuttoning Chris's shorts.

"Why don't you let me take care of the house while you finish the project. I'm off the overtime list. Let me help."

"Oh, you are helping," Luce said as she ran her hands across Chris's naked behind. Luce stopped for a moment. "Is this so we won't have anymore dishwasher moments?"

"Exactly. I can even cook dinner."

"I don't think that's a good idea," Luce said. She took Chris's nipple in her mouth.

Chris found it hard to concentrate but she wanted to get her point across. She would practice restraint. She took Luce's face in her hands. "I'll pick something up. That way, you can get your work done."

"There's another problem," Luce said.

"What's that?"

"I can't stop thinking about you and doing this."

"We'll put you on the incentive program."

"And what does that entail?" Luce ran her hand down Chris's stomach.

Chris quivered. This discussion was getting more difficult by the moment. "You work your brains out—"

"Then you'll fuck me silly when I'm done."

"You're a quick learner."

"I like this plan."

"What did you do before? Let everything go to hell." Chris perched herself on Luce's stomach precariously close to the place where she wanted to go.

"Why do you think I don't have people over very often?"

"Did you eat box food?"

Luce nodded.

"Where's the microwave?"

"It's hidden in the studio. There's a small freezer in there too."

"It all comes out. I like you even better now. That's where Merry Maids and laundry by the pound comes in."

"I have another confession."

"Oh, my, the secret life is deeper than I thought." Chris was slowly grinding against her. She couldn't help it.

"I have a power suit."

"Like the ones B. wears?"

"B. helped me pick it out."

"It's like you're two people. Can I see the suit . . . later?" Chris said as Luce slipped her fingers inside her. The suit would have to wait.

"We could use it for a play night," Luce said.

"I like that even better. You can be the executive and I'll be the secretary."

The next day at lunch Chris went to the Zoo to pick up lunch and have a chat with Amadeus about booking the restaurant for the dance she had planned. She found Amadeus at the bar staring intently and with unabashed infatuation at Elaine. She seemed annoyed to have been caught in the act.

"Hi there. Nice to see you again, Elaine," Chris said.

"Why thank you, Chris," Elaine replied.

"Are you picking up a lunch order?" Amadeus asked.

"Yes, but I also wanted to talk to you about booking the restaurant for an event."

Amadeus raised her eyebrow. "That's an expensive endeavor."

"I know, but you're going to cut me a deal. Besides there will be paying attendees."

"What do you have in mind?" Amadeus took a swig of mineral water.

Chris could tell she was thinking. She didn't want to look bad in front of Elaine, yet commerce was always important.

"I'm planning a ball."

"What?" Amadeus said.

Rose came out with Chris's order of roast beef sandwiches and fries. Chris winked at her. She waved and snuck back to the kitchen.

"A gala ball for midgets. I've invited midgets from all over the United States and about one hundred and twenty-five are coming."

"A midget ball, like tuxes and fancy dresses and Champagne and finger food." Amadeus was clearly skeptical.

"Exactly." Chris watched as Elaine seemed to get it but Amadeus didn't.

"Why would you want to do that?" she asked.

Elaine jumped in, "For Midge. What better way for her to meet a girlfriend? Oh, Chris, that's so nice. I can't believe you found that many."

"The Internet is an amazing place. It took about a month but they want to come. I'm just ironing out the details."

"That's a brilliant idea," Amadeus said. "I can waive the restaurant rental."

"Fabulous. We'll do food and liquor," Chris said.

"Is it a secret?" Amadeus asked.

"Yes, we'll say we're having a fancy evening and then let her rip," Chris said.

"My lips are sealed," Elaine said. "Speaking of which, I better get back to work." She glanced up at the clock.

Amadeus reached across the bar, picked up Elaine's hand and kissed it. "Later?"

"Of course."

Both Chris and Amadeus watched her leave. Her police uniform fit nicely.

"You really like her," Chris said.

"Is it obvious?"

"Yes." Chris plucked a french fry from her lunch bag. "You have the best fries."

"We use a special cooking oil."

Amadeus seemed to want to say something else. Chris waited.

"I want to thank you for making me run into Elaine's police car."

Chris laughed. "You're joking. I'm surprised we're still friends after that. If I remember correctly, the last person who did damage to your car you pressed charges."

"No, really. If not for that I would have missed Elaine."

"So this is serious?"

"I can truly imagine a relationship. We come from similar places."

"She's from Germany." Chris couldn't stop herself.

Amadeus scowled at her.

"I'm sorry."

"I mean she had a long love that went astray and then multiple partners who were all unsatisfying. We are on the same path."

"And she's smart, gorgeous and has a job. All pluses."

Amadeus smiled. "I like when we find common ground."

"It happens once a decade at least."

Later on in the week, B. arranged the closing on Chris's house. She got the VIP treatment because she encouraged a lot of her clients to use this mortgage company. Whatever B. wanted B. got, including the house. Chris was secretly relieved to be done with it. B. was ecstatic.

Chris went to the mortgage office to sign the closing papers. B. and Pippy were already in the lobby. "B., are you sure you want to do this?" She wanted to give her one more chance to get out of it.

"Of course." B. straightened out her copper-colored blazer. It looked suspiciously like the one Amadeus had worn the night of the party.

Chris wondered how she got it. Did B. borrow it from Amadeus or did she get a fabric sample and have it tailored? She wouldn't put it past B. to do either. "I mean, you always thought my house was too small."

"It's Pippy's ancestral home. We don't need much. Your house is perfect for the three of us—less to take care of—and I don't need some status symbol house when I have a family. I want to spend time with them instead of worrying about a housekeeper, a gardener, the pool guy, et cetera."

"Ancestral home?"

"The place where she came into our lives. It's her home and I don't want her to be uprooted."

Chris stopped herself from mentioning that Pippy was a dog. It was a moot point with B. If she wanted Pippy to have her ancestral home, far be it for Chris to stand in the way of their happiness.

Stacey, the mortgage broker that B. always used, came into the reception area. "Hi, B. And you must be Chris," she said, sticking out her hand.

"Nice to meet you," Chris said.

"Come back to my office and we'll get this done," she said.

"You're sure about the price?" B. said. "I don't want you to think you're getting snookered."

"B., we've been through this a hundred times. It's fair."

"Just checking," B. said.

"You would never screw a friend. In fact I think you gave me the better end of the deal."

"No, I didn't. The house has a lot of upgrades and amenities, not to mention its location."

Chris smiled as they entered Stacey's office. B. had thought everything through with her usual precision.

The following Sunday afternoon, Chris, Amadeus and Rose were in kitchen of the Zoo going over the guest list. Amadeus was helping to plan food for the gala event, which was to be held over Columbus Day weekend. Rose, who had done a bang-up job with the championship decorating, was in charge of decorating for the gala ball. She was browsing through catalogs and magazines, trying to get what she called "the picture in her mind" of what the place should look like. Chris was a little alarmed that some of these magazines were bridal ones, thick as encyclopedias. It was all very scary.

The metal doors to the kitchen swung open and like Moses coming down from on high, B. stormed in. "If you're cheating on Luce I'll rip your vagina out with my bare hands. I don't care if it messes up my manicure."

"Me? Cheating. I'm the one that gets cheated on," Chris said.

"Who knows? You could have learned it from the nymphos."

Chris thought the way B. said "nymphos" sounded like they were some uncivilized tribe on the continent of Lesbainia, and like malaria, Chris had been infected.

"Who am I cheating with?" she asked.

"You and Amadeus have been spending a lot of time together," B. said, pointing a long red fingernail at the both of them.

Just then Luce slunk in. She looked mortified, like she'd been unwittingly dragged into this whole mess B. had concocted.

Chris scowled. "Have you lost your fucking mind?" We'd kill each other in the first hour."

This made Amadeus laugh—an infrequent event. "We wouldn't get to bed because we'd be arguing about logistics."

"Exactly. Why did you think I'm cheating?" Chris was suddenly alarmed that this would ever cross Luce's mind.

Luce shrugged. "You said you were going to B.'s. I called to see if we could go to the Range for dinner. You'd left your cell phone on the counter so I called the house. B. hadn't seen you all day. B. tracked down Midge, who said you were with Amadeus earlier." She wasn't looking at Chris but rather studying Amadeus and Rose, who was flipping through magazines like she wished she was anywhere on the planet but here.

"Well, I wasn't exactly lying. I was going over after I was done here."

"Done doing what?" B. asked haughtily. She looked down at the tabletop strewn with magazines, papers and Chris's laptop.

Chris, Amadeus and Rose resembled children caught with their hands in the cookie jar. Chris could tell B. was miffed at being left out of a major planning event. She would have color-coded everything and put it neatly in a leather-bound notebook to be efficiently flipped open at a moment's notice should a question arise or a new idea need to be noted. Actually, they did need her organizational skills. But could they trust her mouth?

"We're planning a gala ball for Midge so she can find a partner," Amadeus said, and as if she wasn't quite certain of the plausibility of the idea, she blamed it on Chris. "It was her idea."

"A midget ball?" B. asked.

"Women from all over are coming," Chris said, tapping her computer.

"Why weren't we informed?" B. asked.

"We wanted to keep it a secret," Chris said meekly.

"Are you saying I can't keep a secret? In case you've forgotten, I was the one that kept your little secret safe," B. said, pointing at her and Luce.

"I was the one that blew it," Luce said.

"I wanted it to be a surprise for everyone but I needed the restaurant."

"We're only in cahoots out of sheer necessity," Amadeus said. Chris should've been insulted but realized Amadeus was only trying to help.

"That is what I consider a marginal excuse," B. said. She looked down at the papers again. "Now, what do we have here? It's a mess."

"Our plans," Chris said.

"Is that what you call it?" B. swooped up papers. She peered over at Rose. "What are you in charge of?"

"Decorations."

"Good. You did a great job for the championship party. Get me your sketches ASAP."

"Yes, ma'am. Rose furiously ripped pages from magazines and quickly scuttled off.

"I think I'll get a bottle of water and see if Rose wants help," Luce said.

"Sure, just leave us to the angry wolf," Chris called out after her.

"Okay, now we're going to organize this into three groupings—food, decorations and music—and then subgroups broken down into specific tasks such as supplies and arrangements. Those in turn . . ."

The rest was lost on Chris. Her eyes glazed over and Amadeus looked much the same. "I have a better idea," she said.

"Really?" B. looked alarmed that she might be outdone by a minion.

"You just tell us what we need to do."

"You want me to be in charge?" B. fluttered her eyelashes as if the idea had never crossed her mind.

"You'd be perfect for it," Amadeus said.

"I completely agree," Chris said.

"Well, I suppose I could help out a little," B. said. "Now, let me see the guest list. I know we get a better rate if we book this at a convention rate. All right, it's September twelfth, we have exactly a month to get this up and rolling. Girls, set your watches and go. Operation Midge-Ball is on."

Chris knew by the time B. was done the gala ball would be perfect. Amadeus put her hands together in prayer and looked upward. Chris seconded the motion.

Chapter Nineteen

"You look absolutely gorgeous tonight," Chris whispered in Luce's ear. She was wearing a silky black dress with a low-cut back. Had Chris not been so busy checking in the guests at the gala ball she would have made sure to find a secluded spot in which to ravish Luce.

"I think you're hot too. I can't believe B. got you into a tux."

"I can't remember what horrible task it got me out of, but I'm sure B. could get the devil to wear Armani."

"Aren't you glad it's finally here?"

"For everyone's sake. I did have to separate B. and Amadeus a few times. Once she almost had B. by the throat."

"Or that one time B. took off her heels and threw them at Amadeus."

"If she hadn't grabbed that frying pan in time she'd be missing an eye," Chris said.

"Two alphas are not safe together."

B.'s voice rang in on the Bluetooth Chris was wearing courtesy of B. She felt like Lieutenant Uhura on *Star Trek*. "The eagle has landed."

"Right. Now, what exactly does that mean?" Chris asked. B. had taken to using cryptic Secret Service language that no one understood but B.

Luce leaned over. "I think it means Midge is here."

B. must have heard her. "Oh, for shit's sake, put someone with skills on. Let me talk to Luce."

Chris plucked the Bluetooth out gladly and handed it to Luce. "She thinks I'm incompetent."

Luce twirled the thing around. Chris had discovered that Luce wasn't very tech-savvy.

"It goes like this," she said, inserting it in Luce's ear.

"I don't like this. It feels like my ear is being violated."

"Violated! Who's getting violated?" B. screamed into the earpiece.

Chris as well as several people around her could hear B. Luce yanked the phone out of her ear. Chris said, "Not so loud, B. You just about blew Luce's ear off. Anyway, we got it. Bring her out in five minutes. We should have everyone in by then."

Chris peeked out the front door. The line of short people had dwindled down to about twenty-five. The traffic was picking up now that there were fewer midgets on the sidewalk. When all one hundred and twenty-five were waiting in line, traffic backed up as people stopped and stared. She'd gone outside with Elaine's bullhorn that Amadeus oddly had in her possession and shyly surrendered. Chris didn't even want to imagine what they were doing with it.

She screamed into the bullhorn, "What, you've never seen midgets before. Have some respect. Pedal to the metal."

That seemed to work for a time, but the slow cars and the gawking picked up again once she went back inside. She induced

Luce's help, and they'd gone to the front to speed the process along.

Amadeus was putting the final touches on the buffet table. They finally decided—or rather, B. decided—that the buffet should be New Mexican because most of the women were from out of town. New Mexican would be exotic and, after all, Midge adored posole. So it was green chili stew, taquitos, shredded beef burritos, margaritas and Mexican beer, of course, plus some local wines. B. was satisfied.

The decorations had gone in the same direction—saddles, pottery, ristras and some Georgia O'Keeffe prints. It looked good, Chris thought. Rose had outdone herself. Gazing across the restaurant-turned-fiesta filled with short gals, she felt the amazing feat they had all achieved. They could never have done it without B. So the honor of announcing the ball had been given to B. Chris was saved the embarrassment of blathering in public. B. would put the right spin on it.

"Is she here?" Amadeus asked as she sidled up to Chris.

"She's in the back with B."

They'd told Midge it was a small dinner party to commemorate B.'s house purchase. It was a thin excuse, but Midge seemed to believe it. Perhaps she'd grown used to B.'s extravaganzas when it came to life's passing moments.

"Is everything ready?" Chris asked.

"Yes, Elaine is helping her DJ friend set up as we speak," Amadeus said.

"The disco ball was a nice touch," Luce said. She took Chris's hand and squeezed it. "This is so exciting."

B. clicked in on the Bluetooth. "All systems go. Commence with Operation Midge-Ball."

Chris rolled her eyes. "Breaker, breaker, gotcha covered, good buddy."

Luce laughed. Amadeus looked mystified.

"What on earth are you talking about?" B. said.

"I don't know. What are you talking about?" Chris replied.

"It's time to bring Midge out."

"We're ready out here."

"Great, but I think we have a little change of plans," B. said. There was some muttering in the background. "Hold on a minute."

"B., what's going on?"

"I'm not comfortable with the blindfold thing. I think you should bring her out. Then I can do the introduction."

"Sure, I'll be right there." Chris hurried back to the kitchen.

B. had duct-taped Midge's leg to the kitchen worktable.

"What have you done to her?" Chris asked.

Midge's face was red and she looked pissed.

"Well, she wouldn't stay put so I had to resort to extraordinary methods."

"So you duct-taped her to a table?"

"I haven't gotten to her hands yet."

"What the hell is going on?" Midge said. She was attempting to unravel the duct tape.

"It's a surprise." B. pulled out her note cards from her breast pocket and quickly reviewed them.

"What kind of a surprise? A bondage party?" Midge was trying to tear the rows of tape with her teeth. B. had been very thorough.

"Where'd you get the tape?" Chris asked.

"I always carry a roll in my purse. A girl never knows when it will come in handy. It works for everything."

"Including tying people up," Midge muttered.

"Wait until we get to the blindfold part," Chris said. She took the silk hanky from B.

"Chris," Midge pleaded.

"Don't worry, you're going to really like this—trust me."

"All right, not long though."

"No. Ten seconds tops."

185

"I can do that," Midge said.

"Okay, cut her loose," Chris said, and B. took a pair of kitchen shears and released her.

Taking a deep breath and straightening her shoulders, B. went out first. Chris led Midge out the swinging kitchen doors. She waited until B. was on the makeshift stage and then she removed the blindfold. There was complete silence.

Midge blinked as though she thought she might be dreaming. "My people," she said.

B. tapped the mike. "Can I have everyone's attention, please. I'd like to officially welcome you all to the first annual people-with-height-challenges gala ball."

"Midgets, we're midgets," the crowd shouted.

Chris gave B. the look. They'd argued over this point. B. was certain the women would be offended.

"All right, midgets, thank you for coming. Let me introduce Sarah K. Roswell, a.k.a Midge."

The spotlight hit Midge, who waved and looked completely overwhelmed until the light was gone and the music started. A Latino beauty whisked her onto the dance floor as the salsa music started.

Jude brought Pippy in. B. was nervous about her being there during the festivities, Jude insisted that Pippy would be heart-broken at being left behind. Jude promised to dog-sit her the entire time. Chris watched as Pippy ran across the room and leapt into B.'s arms. They'd been apart for two hours but they acted like they'd been separated by continents for years. Pippy looked around at all the little people. If a dog's face could say "what the hell," hers did.

B. put her down. "Go look around, but be polite." Pippy went to find Midge.

"Want to dance?" Luce said. She pulled on Chris's hand.

"I'd really like to do some heavy petting in the cloakroom. That dress turns me on."

"That's later."

Chris could see Amadeus and Elaine dancing close and Rose with George wrapped around her. It wasn't hard to pick them out of the sea of short people. Luce ran her hand under Chris's shirt. Chris shivered. "Don't do that."

"You like it," Luce whispered.

"I do."

This was all good, Chris thought. Date Night Club had come to its natural fruition. She was certain of it. She looked over at Midge who was surrounded by a bevy of beauties, the Latina woman included. Midge smiled at Chris and mouthed, "Thank you."

"You're welcome, my friend," Chris replied.

Chapter Twenty

"Why is there so much creamed corn?" George asked.

It was the week before Thanksgiving and the post office was putting on a food drive for one of the local shelters. So far they'd collected a lot of food but not much for a proper holiday dinner.

"Because no one likes creamed corn. We all buy it when it's on sale and it sits in the cupboard because no one likes to throw food away. Giving it away is okay," Chris replied as she sorted through the bags of donated food.

"Yeah, but how are we going to put on a dinner with creamed corn?" George asked.

"Don't forget the canned yams," Mary added as she rifled through another bag.

"And peas. Lots and lots of peas," Gomez said, picking up yet another can.

"Well, we still have a few days," Chris said. She was calculating how many carriers they had working and whether it was time to ask for monetary donations from her fellow postal workers. The yams, peas and corn could work if they came up with some meat. Amadeus had offered two spiral hams but that wasn't going to go far. The shelter figured on about two hundred and fifty people attending the dinner.

"I hope your optimism pays off," Mary said.

"We could always resort to prayer," Chris replied.

"I've got Bible study tonight. We'll give it a try," Mary said.

"Will you put in one for me? Marge is kind of pissed at me," Gomez said.

"Boyfriend, even the Lord can't do much to save your ass from an angry wife," she replied.

Everyone wandered back to their cases as Sid, the supervisor, made a point of looking at his watch.

"Rose misses seeing you at lunch. Even Amadeus has noticed your absence," George said as they walked back to their cases.

"That's because Luce has been packing my lunches with healthy things. I really miss the french fries at the Zoo."

"Can't you go off the good-for-you diet just one day?"

"What'll I do with the lunch? I can't throw it away."

"Gomez will eat anything," George said.

"You're right. I'll go get it from the fridge." Chris looked over her shoulder to see if Sid was still watching them. He must have gone back to his office. "I'll be right back."

"I'll pick up your hot case mail."

"If anyone asks where I am tell them I'm in the can suffering from IBS."

"What's that?"

"Irritable bowel syndrome."

"Yuck!"

"That's why no one wants to know about it."

Chris slinked off to the break room to retrieve her lunch. She handed it to Gomez, who was more than happy to take it.

Chris spent the rest of morning pondering what she'd have for lunch aside from the huge order of french fries.

At lunch Amadeus was actually glad to see her. "Long time no see, stranger."

"Believe me, I've missed the place," Chris said, dipping her pastrami and cheese sandwich in an enormous glob of mustard. She'd already consumed half of her fries.

"Luce is making her lunch," George piped in.

"Still taking your vitamins?" Amadeus said.

"Yes, I'm so healthy now. It's disgusting," Chris whined.

"How's the food drive going?" Rose asked as she refilled their Cokes.

Chris wasn't drinking soda anymore either. She hoped Luce wouldn't find out about her clandestine lunch.

"Sucks," George said.

"Why?" Rose asked.

"Too much creamed corn and no donations for turkey."

"I'll up the ham donations. I've got to order a lot for the holiday," Amadeus said.

"Thanks. That's nice," Chris said. She didn't have the heart to tell her that they needed about fifty hams at this rate. But every little bit helped.

"So is Elaine still working on Thanksgiving?"

"No. She managed a swap. It cost her a hundred dollars but she said that was a small price for spending the holidays with us. Isn't that sweet?"

"That's great," Chris replied, smugly thinking that the word *sweet* wasn't a mainstay in Amadeus's lexicon.

"I'm not completely satisfied with the location. I think your and Luce's house would be more appropriate."

They were having the dinner at B.'s house. Amadeus was obviously still smarting from the gala ball incident when B. tried to nail

190

her with a shoe. Even Chris admitted that was a hostile move. B. did apologize later but Amadeus was one for holding a grudge.

"I know, but B. is still really excited about the house and having her first Thanksgiving there. She has been really *sweet* lately," Chris replied, hoping that using a word straight from Amadeus's new word file would smooth things over.

"For the group, I will make a concession. Christmas is up for negotiation."

"That's fair."

Rose and George were holding hands across the bar and whispering what appeared to be sweet nothings.

"Eat your lunch, George. We've got ten minutes," Chris instructed.

"I know. They gave me a two-hour relay."

"Don't worry. Sid told me I could come help you."

"I like that."

"I got your back, girlfriend."

The next day at work, B. came storming in the backdoor at the post office. "Rose said you're short in the meat department."

"Is that like being short in the pants?" Sanchez asked.

"That's enough out of you, smut-mouth," B. retorted.

"B., you can't be here." Chris snatched a visitor's pass off the supervisor's desk. She slapped it on B.'s lapel.

"No one is having a crappy Thanksgiving on my watch. Chris, we need muscle. I've got Luce's truck and its plum full of *turkeys*." She stared at Sanchez with her one-more-word-out-of-you look. It would be his last. He seemed to get the point.

"But B., the truck from the shelter isn't due until the afternoon," Chris said, nervously looking around. It seemed B.'s presence was causing quite a stir.

George, who was used to the maelstrom B. created, piped up, "The loading dock is pretty cold. The turkeys are frozen, right?"

Chris could tell George regretted asking the question the minute it came out as B. arched her eyebrow in her now famous what-do-I-look-like-a-fucking-moron expression?

"Of course, they're frozen," George replied.

"Now, you two standing there with hands in your pockets—chop-chop. Let's get those *frozen* turkeys on the loading dock." B. pointed at Gomez and Sanchez. They immediately stood at attention.

Sid, drawn by the ruckus, leaned toward Chris. "Would she consider becoming a supervisor? We need someone with her skills."

"Sid, she makes high six figures."

"We could negotiate."

Chris smirked. "You'd sell your soul for someone like her."

Sid smiled. "Souls are overrated."

Sid, it appeared, was not the only one interested in B. Gomez and Sanchez were equally enamored. B. did look stunning in her elegant olive drab Ann Taylor suit complete with low-cut beige blouse.

Sanchez was already at B.'s side awaiting orders. Gomez, who couldn't take his eyes off B.'s amazing bustline stepped across his plastic tubs full of mail and put his foot directly into his small waste can. With his eyes on the prize, he never knew about the waste can.

Chris yelled, "Gomez, watch out!"

Before anyone, including Gomez, could do anything about it, he fell. He tried to catch himself on the side of his case and then crashed onto the floor where he lay writhing in pain. "I think I broke my arm."

His arm was sticking out kind of funny, Chris thought.

B. took immediate charge of the situation. "Oh, you poor man." She scooped him up in her arms, which was quite a task as Gomez was short but substantial. "Medic, we need a medic!"

"My arm, my arm," Gomez cried. He glimpsed B.'s boobs and fainted.

Chris couldn't decide if he fainted from the pain or because he was so close to his favorite part of a woman's anatomy.

"Call nine-one-one," Sid instructed. He studied Gomez's arm. "It's definitely broken." Sid had been a medic in the army.

"I'll bring him back," Sanchez said.

"He fainted. It's not like he needs CPR," Mary said, putting her hands on her hips and shaking her head.

"The ambulance is on its way," Sid said.

"No, really, I got it," Sanchez said. "It's like smelling salts." He reached for his shoe.

George, who'd been casing next to him for a week now, got this queer look of horror on her face. Chris remembered. Sanchez polished his shoes every morning. "That won't be necessary," she said.

"Don't do it, please." George had already plugged her nose.

He did it anyway. He took off his shoe and stuck it under Gomez's nose. Gomez came to immediately, sputtering, "No, not the shoes!"

B. held her nose. "Goodness, haven't you ever heard of Odor Eaters?"

"Put it back on," George said.

Everyone in the vicinity was holding their nose.

"Good God, man, those feet of yours smell worse than Lindberger cheese," Mary said.

"What'd mean? That's a WMD," one of the clerks said.

"Put your shoe back on immediately. That's a direct order," Sid said.

Chris helped B. get Gomez upright. The ambulance drivers arrived and Gomez, much to his dismay, was snatched from B.'s bosom. Once on the stretcher, Chris saw him gaze back at them longingly.

B. shook her head as they carried him away. "Good man gone down."

"Let's get those turkeys unloaded before we have any more mishaps," Chris suggested.

"Yes, we still have a holiday to save," B. said.

They did manage to pull off a decent turkey dinner for the shelter with all the turkeys B. had collected. She had called in all her outstanding favors and then raided the local supermarkets for as many turkeys as would fit in the back of Luce's truck. B. was a little miffed that her organizational skills were stopped at the door. Chris tried to smooth it over by telling B. that the shelter people had been putting on the dinner for years now and they certainly knew best how to conduct it. B. acquiesced, grudgingly.

"Besides, you've got a big enough project just putting on our holiday dinner," Chris said.

"I guess you're right." B. stared at the shelter doors like the Gates of Zion had been shut in her face—a homeland lost forever.

"Don't you have a house to sell?"

"The holidays are kind of slow. But I do have more shopping to do. I best be going."

"Great, see you on Thursday."

B. bustled off and Chris let out a sigh of relief.

On Thursday morning, Chris was standing in the middle of Luce's studio holding a pan of sweet potatoes with a marshmallow-like substance on top. It was Luce's specialty. B. insisted she make it. Chris thought it looked like the kind of food one might see in a PeeWee Herman movie—strangely colored and certainly not edible.

Luce was drilling the wooden frame around a three-by-five

stained-glass piece. She was wearing overalls and safety glasses. Chris was wearing one of Luce's twill aprons. She looked down at herself. The role reversal was not to her liking.

Luce looked up. "You look cute. What's wrong?"

"I feel ridiculous. This thing"—Chris held it out rather distastefully—"is getting all bubbly on top. I kept it in for the allotted time but I don't know if it's done. This is not my gig, you know."

Luce peered over at the pan. "You did all right. It's done. Just set it on the counter to cool."

"Are you almost through?" The studio always fascinated Chris. It was full of tools, most of which Chris had no idea of what they did. There were soldering guns, grip cutters and spools of wires. Those were the tools she could remember. It smelled of wood and the light coming through the skylights and hitting the pieces of colored glass that seemed to be everywhere made her feel like she was in the church of the creative mind.

"Yes. If you'll hold this corner, I can finish the frame and then slap a hanger on it and we're all ready to go."

Chris gladly put the cookware down and held the frame. She liked to help Luce. She was doing a little more around the studio as Luce showed her a few things. It helped to have another set of hands around. Otherwise, Luce had to set up elaborate clamp systems to operate as that extra set of hands.

Luce drilled the last set of screws and attached the hanger. "Now, let's get her wrapped up and crated."

"I can't believe these assholes want it delivered today," Chris said as she helped Luce carefully wrap the piece in a heavy blanket and then gently lay it in the custom-made crate.

"These are rich assholes and my customer wants to show it off to her dinner guests, who are prominent architects."

"So you're putting out for future contracts."

Luce put her goggles back on. "This woman makes B. look like an amateur." She put a few screws into the crate.

Chris took the marshmallow thing back to the kitchen while Luce pulled the truck around. Then they loaded the piece.

"Okay, let's get cleaned up and the holiday begins," Luce said.

"I hope this goes well."

"The drop-off will be quick."

"Not that. B. and Amadeus in the same kitchen."

"Oh, that. I'm sure it'll work itself out."

Chris was not convinced. "You don't sound confident."

"What's a snafu now and then?"

When Luce pulled up in the drive at B.'s house, she asked, "Does it ever feel weird coming here?"

"You mean blood-money house?"

"Yeah."

Chris set the sweet potato thing that she'd carried on her lap to avoid spillage on the console and unbuckled her seat belt. "Not really. It reminds me of how far we've all come. It's like a testimony piece. I mean, we all have life partners now and I think that's amazing."

"I'm really excited to spend some time with Midge's new girl-friend." Luce had been busy getting holiday gift pieces together for the upcoming Christmas art fairs. She hadn't had much time with the group.

"Oh, Juanita is a stitch. She's cute, she's funny and she's well-grounded."

"So she's absolutely perfect for Midge."

"I think so. I've never seen Midge so happy," Chris said. She took a deep breath.

"Ready?" Luce asked.

"Can we say a prayer first?"

"If it'll make you feel better."

Chris took Luce's hand. They closed their eyes and bowed their heads. "Please, let the war of the roses have respite on this day of feasting. Amen."

Luce laughed. "That's a good one."

"Thank you."

Luce carried the hot dish in. Chris opened the front door for her. They could hear Pippy in the backyard barking. She must've been playing with Jude because it was obvious B. and Amadeus were in the kitchen together. They were arguing.

"I knew this wasn't going to work out," Chris said.

"Let's go smooth it over."

As they got closer they could hear the conversation. "I'm telling you, it takes no time for the turkey to cook," Amadeus said. She was going to deep-fry the turkey, which was a new thing.

"Then there should be no problem leaving it in the brine until we put it in the fryer," B. replied.

"It doesn't need to be in brine. The whole purpose of deep frying a turkey is that the juices are sealed in because of the high temperature."

"No one in my family would even think of cooking a turkey without soaking it in brine first," B. replied.

Chris and Luce stood in the hallway. "Do we really want to go in there?" Chris knew when B. brought up her family it was the beginning of the war. The guns were in lock-and-load position.

"We have to," Luce said. She walked in the kitchen first.

It all happened so fast that no one had any time to react. Amadeus and B. were having a tug-of-war with the turkey. B. had stored the turkey in a cooler full of ice water and brine. She was trying to put it back in the ice chest and Amadeus was attempting to rescue it from further brining. Together, they managed to knock over the cooler and send the turkey flying across the room. It hit Luce in the shins and she landed face-first in the pan of sweet potatoes. Chris tried to help her but the ice cubes from the cooler combined with all the water made the kitchen floor like an ice skating rink. Chris went down. B. landed hard on her butt and Amadeus, who'd been exerting the most force on the turkey, went sailing across the floor until her head hit the refrigerator and she came to an abrupt stop.

Luce looked up at Chris. "Maybe you were right."

Chris scooped a finger full of the hot dish off Luce's face. "This stuff isn't half bad."

B. glared at Amadeus, who glared back.

Luce interceded. "I think we've had enough altercations for one day. The turkey can be rinsed off and the floor cleaned."

"All right," B. said.

Pippy must have heard the ruckus. She came flying in the kitchen with Jude in tow. She barked as she slid across the floor, unable to get any traction. She eventually slid into B.'s lap.

Jude didn't say a word. Of course, she'd been there all morning and had seen most of what was going on. She took the digital camera B. had bought her for her birthday from her breast pocket and photo-documented the event.

This made B. laugh. Then they all laughed, even Amadeus. They were laughing so hard that they didn't have time to avert the second set of mishaps.

"You guys sound like you're having a blast in here," Midge said.

"Midge, don't come in here!" Chris yelled.

It was too late. "Why not?" Midge said, as her boot slipped on an ice cube. She tried to save Juanita. They spun around like they were waltzing until Midge fell on top of Juanita. "This wasn't how I imagined our first intimate moment," Midge said as she lay between Juanita's legs.

"Me either."

Midge saw the turkey wedged under the kitchen bar. "What happened to the turkey?"

"It was abducted by aliens and turned into a secret weapon. It was programmed to attack holiday diners," Chris said as she scooted on her butt over to the broom closet. They were going to have to get this ice off the floor or someone was really going to get hurt.

"That's what it looks like," Juanita said. Midge pulled her to a sitting position. No one stood up yet.

"I'd wager on two alphas in the kitchen," Midge said.

"And you'd be right." Luce pulled a kitchen towel off the rack and was trying to get the sweet potato off her face. Chris offered to lick it. "I don't think so."

Before Chris could make it to the broom closet, B. took charge. "Jude, get the wet dry vac from the garage and we'll vacuum this up."

"I'm on it."

After forty-five minutes, the kitchen floor was dried, the turkey cleaned up and in the deep fryer and they were sipping wine in the living room. It almost looked like a normal holiday gathering except they were all wearing robes—B.'s robes. Midge and Juanita wore brightly colored silk kimonos. Luce and Chris had matching white terrycloth ones. Chris thought they looked like they were at the day spa. B. and Jude, who out of solidarity opted for a robe as well, had matching flannel plaid ones. B., in an effort to mend fences with Amadeus, gave her a beautiful full-length gold lamé robe. Amadeus looked amazing in it, like she was a goddess straight from the island of Lesbos.

"I must say, this is the most amusing holiday I've ever had," Juanita said. She was the stunning Latina woman who had asked Midge to dance first at the gala ball. They'd been tight ever since. Chris was convinced they were soul mates. So was Midge.

"Just keep hanging around with us and it'll get better," Chris said.

There was a knock at the door and Amadeus got up to answer it. It was Elaine. She was holding a dozen yellow roses she'd brought for the table centerpiece. She looked at them and then at her own outfit of a brown blazer and dress pants.

"Believe me, yours is more suitable," Amadeus assured her.

"What happened?" Elaine asked.

"Come have some wine and we'll tell you the whole sordid tale," Chris said.

Publications from
BELLA BOOKS, INC.
The best in contemporary lesbian fiction

P.O. Box 10543, Tallahassee, FL 32302
Phone: 800-729-4992
www.bellabooks.com

OUT OF THE FIRE by Beth Moore. Author Ann Covington feels at the top of the world when told her book is being made into a movie. Then in walks Casey Duncan the actress who is playing the lead in her movie. Will Casey turn Ann's world upside down?
1-59493-088-0 $13.95

STAKE THROUGH THE HEART: NEW EXPLOITS OF TWILIGHT LESBIANS by Karin Kallmaker, Julia Watts, Barbara Johnson and Therese Szymanski. The playful quartet that penned the acclaimed *Once Upon A Dyke* are dimming the lights for journeys into worlds of breathless seduction.   1-59493-071-6 $15.95

THE HOUSE ON SANDSTONE by KG MacGregor. Carly Griffin returns home to Leland and finds that her old high school friend Justine is awakening more than just old memories.   1-59493-076-7 $13.95

WILD NIGHTS: MOSTLY TRUE STORIES OF WOMEN LOVING WOMEN edited by Therese Szymanski. 264 pp. 23 new stories from today's hottest erotic writers are sure to give you your wildest night ever!   1-59493-069-4 $15.95

COYOTE SKY by Gerri Hill. 248 pp. Sheriff Lee Foxx is trying to cope with the realization that she has fallen in love for the first time. And fallen for author Kate Winters, who is technically unavailable. Will Lee fight to keep Kate in Coyote?   1-59493-065-1 $13.95

VOICES OF THE HEART by Frankie J. Jones. 264 pp. A series of events force Erin to swear off love as she tries to break away from the woman of her dreams. Will Erin ever find the key to her future happiness?   1-59493-068-6 $13.95

SHELTER FROM THE STORM by Peggy J. Herring. 296 pp. A story about family and getting reacquainted with one's past that shows that sometimes you don't appreciate what you have until you almost lose it.   1-59493-064-3 $13.95

WRITING MY LOVE by Claire McNab. 192 pp. Romance writer Vonny Smith believes she will be able to woo her editor Diana through her writing . . .   1-59493-063-5 $13.95

PAID IN FULL by Ann Roberts. 200 pp. Ari Adams will need to choose between the debts of the past and the promise of a happy future.   1-59493-059-7 $13.95

ROMANCING THE ZONE by Kenna White. 272 pp. Liz's world begins to crumble when a secret from her past returns to Ashton . . .   1-59493-060-0 $13.95

SIGN ON THE LINE by Jaime Clevenger. 204 pp. Alexis Getty, a flirtatious delivery driver is committed to finding the rightful owner of a mysterious package.
1-59493-052-X $13.95

END OF WATCH by Clare Baxter. 256 pp. LAPD Lieutenant L.A Franco Frank follows the lone clue down the unlit steps of memory to a final, unthinkable resolution.
1-59493-064-4 $13.95

BEHIND THE PINE CURTAIN by Gerri Hill. 280 pp. Jacqueline returns home after her father's death and comes face-to-face with her first crush.
1-59493-057-0 $13.95

PIPELINE by Brenda Adcock. 240 pp. Joanna faces a lost love returning and pulling her into a seamy underground corporation that kills for money.
1-59493-062-7 $13.95

18TH & CASTRO by Karin Kallmaker. 200 pp. First-time couplings and couples who know how to mix lust and love make 18th & Castro the hottest address in the city by the bay.
1-59493-066-X $13.95

JUST THIS ONCE by KG MacGregor. 200 pp. Mindful of the obligations back home that she must honor, Wynne Connelly struggles to resist the fascination and allure that a particular woman she meets on her business trip represents.
1-59493-087-2 $13.95

ANTICIPATION by Terri Breneman. 240 pp. Two women struggle to remain professional as they work together to find a serial killer.
1-59493-055-4 $13.95

OBSESSION by Jackie Calhoun. 240 pp. Lindsey's life is turned upside down when Sarah comes into the family nursery in search of perennials.
1-59493-058-9 $13.95

BENEATH THE WILLOW by Kenna White. 240 pp. A torch that still burns brightly even after twenty-five years threatens to consume two childhood friends.
1-59493-053-8 $13.95

SISTER LOST, SISTER FOUND by Jeanne G'fellers. 224 pp. The highly anticipated sequel to No Sister of Mine.
1-59493-056-2 $13.95

THE WEEKEND VISITOR by Jessica Thomas. 240 pp. In this latest Alex Peres mystery, Alex is asked to investigate an assault on a local woman but finds that her client may have more secrets than she lets on.
1-59493-054-6 $13.95

THE KILLING ROOM by Gerri Hill. 392 pp. How can two women forget and go their separate ways?
1-59493-050-3 $12.95

PASSIONATE KISSES by Megan Carter. 240 pp. Will two old friends run from love?
1-59493-051-1 $12.95

ALWAYS AND FOREVER by Lyn Denison. 224 pp. The girl next door turns Shannon's world upside down.
1-59493-049-X $12.95

BACK TALK by Saxon Bennett. 200 pp. Can a talk show host find love after heartbreak?
1-59493-028-7 $12.95

THE PERFECT VALENTINE: EROTIC LESBIAN VALENTINE STORIES edited by Barbara Johnson and Therese Szymanski—from Bella After Dark. 328 pp. Stories from the hottest writers around.
1-59493-061-9 $14.95

MURDER AT RANDOM by Claire McNab. 200 pp. The Sixth Denise Cleever Thriller. Denise realizes the fate of thousands is in her hands.
1-59493-047-3 $12.95

THE TIDES OF PASSION by Diana Tremain Braund. 240 pp. Will Susan be able to hold it all together and find the one woman who touches her soul?   1-59493-048-1 $12.95

JUST LIKE THAT by Karin Kallmaker. 240 pp. Disliking each other—and everything they stand for—even before they meet, Toni and Syrah find feelings can change, just like that.
1-59493-025-2 $12.95

WHEN FIRST WE PRACTICE by Therese Szymanski. 200 pp. Brett and Allie are once again caught in the middle of murder and intrigue.   1-59493-045-7 $12.95

REUNION by Jane Frances. 240 pp. Cathy Braithwaite seems to have it all: good looks, money and a thriving accounting practice . . .   1-59493-046-5 $12.95

BELL, BOOK & DYKE: NEW EXPLOITS OF MAGICAL LESBIANS by Kallmaker, Watts, Johnson and Szymanski. 360 pp. Reluctant witches, tempting spells and skyclad beauties—delve into the mysteries of love, lust and power in this quartet of novellas.
1-59493-023-6 $14.95

ARTIST'S DREAM by Gerri Hill. 320 pp. When Cassie meets Luke Winston, she can no longer deny her attraction to women . . .   1-59493-042-2 $12.95

NO EVIDENCE by Nancy Sanra. 240 pp. Private Investigator Tally McGinnis once again returns to the horror-filled world of a serial killer.   1-59493-043-04 $12.95

WHEN LOVE FINDS A HOME by Megan Carter. 280 pp. What will it take for Anna and Rona to find their way back to each other again?   1-59493-041-4 $12.95

MEMORIES TO DIE FOR by Adrian Gold. 240 pp. Rachel attempts to avoid her attraction to the charms of Anna Sigurdson . . .   1-59493-038-4 $12.95

SILENT HEART by Claire McNab. 280 pp. Exotic lesbian romance.

1-59493-044-9 $12.95

MIDNIGHT RAIN by Peggy J. Herring. 240 pp. Bridget McBee is determined to find the woman who saved her life.   1-59493-021-X $12.95

THE MISSING PAGE A Brenda Strange Mystery by Patty G. Henderson. 240 pp. Brenda investigates her client's murder . . .   1-59493-004-X $12.95

WHISPERS ON THE WIND by Frankie J. Jones. 240 pp. Dixon thinks she and her best friend, Elizabeth Colter, would make the perfect couple . . .   1-59493-037-6 $12.95

CALL OF THE DARK: EROTIC LESBIAN TALES OF THE SUPERNATURAL edited by Therese Szymanski—from Bella After Dark. 320 pp.   1-59493-040-6 $14.95

A TIME TO CAST AWAY A Helen Black Mystery by Pat Welch. 240 pp. Helen stops by Alice's apartment—only to find the woman dead . . .   1-59493-036-8 $12.95

DESERT OF THE HEART by Jane Rule. 224 pp. The book that launched the most popular lesbian movie of all time is back.   1-1-59493-035-X $12.95

THE NEXT WORLD by Ursula Steck. 240 pp. Anna's friend Mido is threatened and eventually disappears . . .   1-59493-024-4 $12.95

CALL SHOTGUN by Jaime Clevenger. 240 pp. Kelly gets pulled back into the world of private investigation . . .   1-59493-016-3 $12.95

52 PICKUP by Bonnie J. Morris and E.B. Casey. 240 pp. 52 hot, romantic tales—one for every Saturday night of the year.   1-59493-026-0 $12.95